David Catesby is a chartered accountant who has lived and practised in Britain and North America.

He read somewhere that everyone has one good book in them. He says that he hopes that the statement is true, and that writing this book absolves him from writing any more, in case he develops the dreaded writer's block, which mercifully never afflicted him while writing this one.

An Innocent Obsession

David Catesby

An Innocent Obsession

Chimera

CHIMERA PAPERBACK

© Copyright 2005
David Catesby

The right of David Catesby to be identified as author of
this work has been asserted by him in accordance with the
Copyright, Designs and Patents Act 1988

All Rights Reserved

No reproduction, copy or transmission of this publication
may be made without written permission.
No paragraph of this publication may be reproduced,
copied or transmitted save with the written permission or in
accordance with the provisions
of the Copyright Act 1956 (as amended).

Any person who does any unauthorised act in relation to
this publication may be liable to criminal
prosecution and civil claims for damage.

A CIP catalogue record for this title is
available from the British Library
ISBN 1 903136 32 6

Chimera is an imprint of
Pegasus Elliot MacKenzie Publishers Ltd.
www.pegasuspublishers.com

First Published in 2005

Chimera
Sheraton House Castle Park
Cambridge England

Printed & Bound in Great Britain

Dedication

With love to Kate, who should
have written this book had she lived.

PREFACE

The death of my wife Kate in an accident brought to a premature end a very happy marriage. When I could bring myself to go through her things I found in the bottom of her wardrobe a battered binder containing notes from her days as a nursing student, other notes written later and a diary recording her first pregnancy and early days as a mother.

She had been editor of the nursing school gazette and had a gift for writing but I had never seen any of this material. In one place in the diary she muses on showing it or reading it to me one day, but sadly she went out in the prime of life and we never had the fun – for that's what it would have been – of reading it together or, what I would have loved, her reading it to me.

As I have said ours was a very happy marriage. We were a very compatible couple. I was Kate's first and only boyfriend and she was my first and only girlfriend. She was a rather reserved girl, but within our marriage she was an enthusiastic and uninhibited lover – a delight to know and be married to.

Soon after we became engaged Kate read in a magazine an item on the topic of acucullophilia which she discovered was the technical term for a woman attracted to circumcised men. Kate had been brought up by a mother, also a nurse, who believed that all males should be circumcised at birth and had encouraged Kate in this belief. On reading the article Kate promptly diagnosed herself as an acucullophiliac, an appellation she gleefully adopted and revealed to me that same day. Her enthusiasm certainly did no harm to our relationship - luckily my mother held similar views to Kate's mother so I was acceptable to Kate – and I have no doubt that Kate's enthusiasm or obsession, call it what one will, had the effect of greatly enhancing our life together.

Some may say that my account of life with Kate is too

intimate for publication but I think Kate, a highly professional and conscientious nurse, would see my publishing it as propagating and keeping alive her belief in the benefits of male circumcision in an era when circumcision has been virtually eradicated in Britain due to a cost cutting diktat of the National Health Service, although it remains a common practice in the free enterprise culture of American medical practice, the United States being a country in which individual freedom is more cherished than in Britain.

In Britain, soon after the creation of the National Health Service, it banned circumcision on parental request, a request often made and acted on in pre-NHS Britain and one still honoured as a matter of course in the United States and Canada.

I believe that this book is timely because since Kate's death there have been four developments which make publication of her views on the benefits of circumcision particularly opportune.

First, recent research in Africa into the mechanism by which men become infected by the virus which causes HIV leading to AIDS has shown that a circumcised man is much less vulnerable to infection than his intact counterpart. Assuming the validity of this research the National Health Service ban on circumcision may have had tragic consequences for some British AIDS victims.

Secondly, in some areas of Britain with a significant Muslim population the National Health Service has quietly reversed its anti-circumcision stance by providing hospital facilities for circumcision. The new policy discriminates against non-Muslim parents who, at least in other areas of Britain, are presumably still routinely met with refusal when they request circumcision for their sons.

Thirdly, the rise of vociferous anti-circumcision activists, particularly on the internet.

Fourthly, the opening in Britain of privately funded clinics offering circumcision.

Published at a time when the National Health Service is in the throes of reform and, one may hope, some such needed introspection and is at last paying lip-service to the importance of client satisfaction, this book may give encouragement to those who believe the National Health Service should now review its 50 year old ban and extend its facilities to all parents, irrespective of their race or religious affiliation, who wish to have their sons circumcised.

But primarily this book is a celebration of the happiness of our marriage and a tribute to a wonderful wife, lover, companion and friend.

Prologue

Soliloquy

Kate was enjoying the luxury of a late night bath at home following a hard day's slog at the nursing school where she was a first year student.

Her parents and her two brothers had gone to bed and she had seized the opportunity this offered of a relaxing soak in a hot bath without any serious likelihood of anyone hammering on the door and claiming she was hogging the bathroom – a frequent complaint of her brothers, both younger than her.

Kate was a quiet, reserved girl, regarded as a very good student both at the girls' school she had attended until recently and at the nursing school; interested and absorbed in the courses she was taking and looking forward to her chosen career in nursing. She was a good looking girl, fair haired, slim and well-proportioned.

She was lying full length in the bath, only her head above water, very relaxed in the warm water, revelling in the solitude and peace and musing on how enjoyable her life was compared with many others. Yes, she thought, she was fortunate in her family and being able to make a start in a profession which she chosen for herself without any pressure from her parents.

As time passed she became drowsy and her thought processes slowed. Rather dreamily she began to think that perhaps she was missing out on one thing - unlike, she thought, probably every other student in the nursing school, she didn't have a boyfriend. She had listened for months to the other student nurses chattering away about their boyfriends and even fiancés, as some no older than she were already engaged. At her girls' boarding school during term time she and her fellow pupils were sedulously segregated from boys and during the school holidays her brothers and their friends excluded her from most of their activities so she had had little chance of meeting boys and she felt isolated from them. Recently she had begun to feel a little envious when other girls talked about their boyfriends.

Still drowsy she fell to wondering, as she had often done recently, what having a boyfriend would be like and what it would be like to be married. What would it be like to make love and have love made to her? Was it all that her fellow students made it out to be? What would it feel like to be kissed passionately? And to have her breasts caressed and her nipples kissed? From that starting point she began to wonder how she would react to some boy she really liked making real love to her.

Kate's parents had always been very forthcoming over the facts of life with all their children and as a result, long before she went to nursing school she was very knowledgeable for one of her age about sexual matters. She was satisfied that she had a sound theoretical knowledge even though she was totally lacking in practical experience.

She would like to meet a boy about the same age as herself, perhaps a student at the university with which the hospital and its nursing school were affiliated. She would like someone intelligent with intellectual interests, coming from a professional background like her own family's and sufficiently industrious and ambitious that by their combined efforts they could create a good future together if they married. She hoped he would be slim, healthy and reasonably good looking. But he needn't be a sports jock – no, he certainly must not be one – she didn't want someone whose idea of a good Saturday afternoon was playing rugger, soccer or cricket or, even worse, spending long hours on a sofa watching sports on television. If he was going to spend leisure time on a sofa she thought he should be sharing the sofa with her, not passing the time with spectator sports but instead in making love or, better still, engaging in the preliminaries thereto before he carried her off to a comfortable bed for the rest of the afternoon.

The thought of making love propelled her, tired though she was, into trying to imagine the emotional and physical sensations that she would experience when, not if she reminded herself firmly, she met someone she loved and who loved her. She knew a great deal about the anatomy, male as well as female, of lovemaking, but what would it actually feel like to be totally nude with one's lover for the first time when each was able to see, feel and embrace the other's naked body? How would he react to a nude Kate? Would he be turned on by her body? Would she be turned on by his? How would she react to the first sight of his erect penis knowing that it was about to enter her? And, more to the point, how would it feel to yield her virginity to her lover, who she hoped would be gentle and patient with her, and feel his erect penis entering and then filling the cavity of her vagina before bringing her to orgasm?

These musings led to her moving her legs apart and touching, very gently, her clitoris which responded to her mood and her caress. Then, very tentatively, she pushed her forefinger past her hymen into her vagina and tried to imagine that it was a penis. A very small penis, she said to herself, and she hoped that when one did enter her it would be larger, but not too large, and would be moved within her with sufficient skill and vigour to bring her to climax, but not with so much vigour as to cause discomfort rather than the pleasure she hoped her lover would give her.

Sexually aroused as she was, but sleepier than ever now, she tried to visualize the penis of her ideal lover. She knew that size – within limits – was not nearly as important as the way in which the penis was used. On one matter she was adamant. Because of her views on the importance of hygiene and her own sexual and aesthetic preferences, any man making love to her must have a circumcised penis, a tightly circumcised one with only enough skin left to allow its full erection. She tried to imagine this ideal penis in both its erect and flaccid states, but the effort was too much for someone as sleepy as by now she had become. She gave up the attempt and lay relaxed in the warmth of the bath.

Chapter 1

Kate's Childhood

Kate's upbringing had been different from most as after World War II her parents spent several years in the Middle East and she and her brother, who was younger than she was, had accompanied their mother, Mary, when she joined Kate's father there after the war ended. Her father had had what was called a "good war." An electrical engineer who was convinced that war was imminent, he had volunteered to join the Royal Naval Volunteer Reserve in July 1939 although he was in a reserved occupation which exempted him from call up and despite the fact that he was married with two young children. He was granted an immediate commission and soon afterwards was selected for specialist training on magnetic mines. Thereafter he undertook the dangerous work of deactivating German mines of this type. Later he commanded a minesweeper in the Mediterranean. At the end of the war the Admiralty decided to establish an Electrical Branch and, due to his qualifications as an electrical engineer, including a first class honours degree, and his distinguished and wide ranging war record, he had been identified by the Admiralty as one whose future career was likely to take him to the top of the new Branch. So considerable pressure was put on him to accept a permanent commission in the post-war Navy but, although he agreed to stay on for a while to help in the huge and risky task of clearing the enormous number of mines laid in and around the Mediterranean by both sides during the war, he was anxious to return to civilian life so that he wouldn't lose his niche in a highly competitive profession.

As the Navy was so anxious to retain his services he was quite shameless in demanding a quid pro quo and this resulted in his being allowed very soon after VE Day to bring his wife and their two children to Egypt to join him in Alexandria where he was then based. As a birthday treat Kate was taken to see the Pyramids and this began what was for her a wonderful period when her father's work took her and her family to a variety of interesting places and instilled in her a love of the Middle East and a yen for travel which she was never to lose.

It was in Alexandria that she came home one day from the British run school she attended and noticed an unusual Royal Navy cap hanging on the hat rack in the hall. She knew it wasn't her father's as the one on the peg had gold oak leaves on its peak and Lieutenant Commanders like Daddy didn't rate what she knew was called a "brass hat." She wondered who was visiting but the dining room and lounge were empty. She found her mother in the kitchen and asked who the visitor was. "No one's visiting, dear. Why do you ask?" "There's a brass hat hung up in the hall." Her mother smiled proudly. "Oh, that's Daddy's new hat, dear. He's been promoted to Commander. We're taking you and John out to a restaurant tonight to celebrate. Now go and put your blue dress on and get ready."

Kate's mother had told her that soon she would have another little brother or a sister and Kate was taking a lot of interest in her mother's pregnancy. Both her parents were very open with their children about reproduction and sex and she knew that any questions she asked would always be answered fully and frankly and in language that she could understand.

Kate hadn't seen much of her father during the war as he had been away in the Mediterranean for most of it. Shortly before VE Day he received a temporary posting in Britain and the family moved to temporary digs near his posting so that they could be together for a while. It was then that Kate and John got to know again the father they had hardly seen for nearly five years. It was odd at first to have a near stranger in the family home but they got on well and Kate and her brother came to love him for his gentle ways and the interesting things he talked about and showed them. It was during this interlude that Kate's mother, like so many other women whose husbands had been away at the war for years, became pregnant and it was as an expectant mum that Mary had boarded the troopship that was to take her and her two children to Egypt to join her husband. Kate loved that voyage. Her mother took every advantage of calls in ports en route to show her children interesting places and sights.

In Alexandria Kate quickly made new friends at school while her mother took her place in the community of British service wives and rapidly formed new friendships. After the other service wives found out that Mary was a highly qualified nurse who had been an operating theatre sister they came to look to her for advice as they faced the challenges of raising families in an alien climate. Mary enjoyed the contacts with so many new acquaintances and once she accepted the role thrust on her, she came to find the challenges – and they were many, varied and frequent – that she had to deal with very rewarding. Some service wives were bored; Mary never had the time or opportunity to become bored and she was very happy in her new environment.

One of the naval wives she became particularly friendly with was Joan, who had a daughter in Kate's class at school and a year old son. Joan and her two children had travelled to Alexandria aboard the same troopship as Mary and they became well acquainted during the voyage. With a small baby to look after, Joan found shore excursions en route difficult and tiring and usually her daughter went ashore with Mary and her family leaving Joan and the baby on board. Joan found life in Alexandria raised more day to day problems than did her former life among the other naval wives in Southsea and she worried particularly about her children; she found Mary a tower of strength in helping her sort out the myriad problems that seemed to beset her. Both mothers visited each other's houses almost on a daily basis and took their children along with them unless they were in school.

Morning coffee was a favourite excuse for a visit and

during school holidays, Kate and John would go with Mary to Joan's. On occasion, when Mary arrived with her children for coffee, she found Joan in a state of anxiety about the baby. Joan explained that while bathing him that morning she had attempted to wash his genital area but he had started to cry and was obviously in pain. She told Mary that his "little pee-pee" looked very red and she thought he might have some sort of infection. Would Mary have a look and tell her if she thought she should take him to the naval base doctor? "Of course I will," said Mary. Joan took his nappy off and put him on Mary's lap so that she could examine him. Seeing immediately that the end of his penis was inflamed she asked Joan how long the condition had lasted and was told that the first time she had noticed the redness was that morning when she had taken him from his cot to change his nappy. She hesitated a bit as if embarrassed before asking if Mary thought the inflammation might be related to the fact that although she had tried very gently to pull his foreskin back in the bath occasionally to check whether it had loosened sufficiently to be retractable, she had never been able to do more than expose "the little hole he pees through." She told Mary that staff at the hospital where the baby had been born had told her not to expect his foreskin to become retractable before the age of three and that in no circumstances should she try to pull it back until it moved freely, and she had followed this advice. She had asked in the hospital whether he should be circumcised as some of her friends' babies had been and was told it wasn't necessary; she should let nature take its course and not worry about his foreskin not being retractable. If she couldn't easily pull it back by the age of six then she should take him to her doctor who would decide if a circumcision was advisable.

Mary said she was pretty sure the baby had an infection under his foreskin but she couldn't be certain without pulling the skin back as far as it would go and with the inflamed state of his penis that would hurt him. Because any examination would be painful the fewer examinations he had the better. Joan should take him to the doctor who would have to examine him. If Mary tried to examine him as well as the doctor the baby would suffer pain twice and once was enough.

Kate had watched her mother examining the baby and was puzzled by what she had seen and heard. After they got home she asked, "Mum, why does Joan's baby's penis look different from John's? It's all covered with skin and it doesn't have a rounded end like an acorn like John has." Her mother explained, "Joan's little boy has skin covering his penis called a foreskin. Every little boy is born like that and John was, but after John was born we asked the doctor to cut away enough skin to expose the rounded end of his penis which was hidden under the foreskin. The cutting of the foreskin is called circumcision and we asked the doctor to circumcise John a few days after he was born because it makes it a lot easier to keep the penis clean. Joan's baby was not circumcised. If he had been circumcised he wouldn't have a foreskin to get an infection under. After Joan has taken the baby to the doctor she's probably going to wish that he had been circumcised at birth like John, as it's likely that sooner or later her baby will have to be circumcised and doing a circumcision later is much harder on the baby and on his mother, too."

Joan took her baby to the doctor soon after Mary left. The doctor examined the baby and confirmed that he had an infection under the foreskin. He would prescribe an antibiotic which should clear it up, but there was a danger of future infections. He told Joan that once the present infection had been cleared up they could wait and see whether he got any more infections. If he got another, Joan and her husband should think about having the baby circumcised.

The antibiotic cleared the infection up, but a few weeks later the baby developed another infection under his foreskin which again required treatment with an antibiotic. After this Joan sought Mary's advice. Joan said she and her husband thought that the baby should be circumcised and now wished they had arranged to have it done while she and the baby were still in the maternity hospital after the birth. Mary said that if she were in Joan's shoes, she would ask for him to be circumcised as soon as the present infection had been cleared up. Joan thanked her and said she was going to arrange for his circumcision.

A week later Joan phoned and told Mary that an appointment had been made for the operation to be performed and that the baby would be in the hospital for the night following surgery and discharged the next day. Mary went with Joan and the baby when he was admitted. Joan was weeping when she left the ward after tucking her son up in his cot and Mary was glad that she had invited Joan to spend the day with her at her home. Mary asked the admitting nurse to phone Joan at Mary's house as soon as the baby had been returned to the ward after surgery. Mary spent the intervening time doing all she could to reassure Joan that she had made the right decision, but Joan remained upset and occasionally tearful until the call came through that the operation had been performed, the baby was doing well and he could be picked up the next morning.

The next day Kate and John left with their parents on a two week holiday trip up the Nile. A few days after their return, Mary took Kate to visit Joan at her home and Joan asked Mary if she would look at the baby's penis and tell her if she thought the surgeon had done a good job. Joan removed the baby's nappy and Mary was able to tell her that she thought the operation had been performed satisfactorily and he was healing well.

Joan seemed relieved at this and remarked, "You know, with hindsight, it would have been so much better if he had been circumcised immediately after birth. Some of my friends who had baby boys arranged for circumcisions to be done before they left the nursing home or hospital and I wish now I had listened to their advice and done the same. Having it done later is much harder on the baby and a lot more worrying for the parents. Mary, do you mind my asking if you had John circumcised and whether you plan to have your new baby done if it's a boy?"

Mary told Joan that her hospital experience had included some time in maternity and paediatric departments before she moved into theatre work and she had seen and assisted at many circumcisions of newborns and older boys and had cared for both circumcised and uncircumcised boys in the paediatric department. As a student, she had also nursed adult males in the general and surgical wards. She had formed her own opinions about the advisability or otherwise of circumcision as a result of her own broad experience. Rightly or wrongly, she had decided that any son of hers would be circumcised soon after his birth and her husband had agreed with her, so John had been circumcised before she took him home from the nursing home where he was born. For John she had engaged the services of a surgeon whom she had assisted at several circumcisions and whose skill and care in doing the operation she had observed and admired. If her new baby was a boy he too would be circumcised, but this time she would not be able to select a surgeon whose work she was familiar with and she was going to make inquiries of doctors, nurses and mothers of young sons and seek recommendations.

When her mother had been examining Joan's baby, Kate could see that the cap of skin over the end of his penis had been removed and she saw the rounded end which had previously been hidden by skin and was now fully exposed to view. There was a reddish line round his penis below the rounded end. Kate waited until she was in the car being driven home before she started to ask questions. She asked if the baby had had an anaesthetic and, told that he had, she asked if he would have felt any pain after it wore off. She commented that the baby's penis – her parents encouraged both their children to use the correct words rather than euphemisms – now looked like her brother's except for the red line round it, and Mary explained that the redness would disappear when the wound had healed completely. Kate said that she thought the baby's penis looked much nicer now than before. When she was in the bath with John, her mother always washed his penis and she couldn't understand how Joan could have kept her baby clean if she couldn't pull the skin back to clean the round bit at the end of his penis. Mary gulped slightly at the acuity of this analysis and said that Kate was quite right, but added it wasn't quite as important in a small baby as in an older boy or man. Kate said that she was pleased to have seen the baby's penis before and after the circumcision, stumbling slightly as she tried to pronounce the long word, as she now realized there were two types of penis and now understood why they looked different.

Kate asked why her mother and father had decided before her brother was born to have him circumcised. Mary told her that it was easier to keep a penis clean if it had been circumcised, and also it was better for a woman if her husband had been circumcised because she benefited from the greater cleanliness of his penis when it entered her vagina when they were making babies. If a baby was circumcised when he was newly born, it was a simpler and quicker operation and healed faster than if it was done later and although a newborn baby wasn't anaesthetised and suffered pain, he didn't remember it. She said that she agreed with Kate's observation that a circumcised penis looked better than one that hadn't been circumcised.

Kate asked her about the new baby. Because of what she had heard her mother say to Joan, she knew that if it was a boy he was going to be circumcised. But her mother had said she hadn't decided yet who would do the operation. Yet her mother knew a lot of doctors in Alexandria. Joan had been able to find a doctor to operate on her baby. Why was her mother having difficulty in finding a doctor to circumcise the new baby? Mary explained that because of her nursing experience she knew that some doctors did much better and neater circumcisions than others and, if (she laid heavy emphasis on the "if ") she had another baby boy she wanted him to have as skilled an operator as John had had. If she couldn't find a good one in Alexandria they would wait until they returned home and ask the same surgeon who had done such a neat circumcision on John to operate on her second son. As Mary parked outside her house, Kate asked her mother to let her see the new baby's penis before he was circumcised and show her how the operation would be done.

Before they got out of the car Mary said cheerfully, "Of course, if you get a sister we won't have to worry about circumcision, anyway."

Mary had been surprised and impressed by the amount of

thought which had gone into Kate's questions and how much she had observed and had absorbed from the conversation between Joan and herself. She already knew that Kate was a highly intelligent girl, but it was now obvious to her that Kate was very interested in medical matters and this might be a pointer to her long term future.

Although the doctors at the naval base hospital were competent practitioners, there was no specialist in obstetrics or paediatrics among them and Mary decided to investigate whether the doctors serving the European community in Alexandria could offer better care than the naval base hospital for the birth.

She and her husband had come to know some of the cosmopolitan business community, which included some very wealthy people indeed, but what she could not find were any British or American trained obstetricians or paediatricians. She could not return to Britain for the birth as space on ships bound for Britain was reserved for service personnel as she had been warned before she left Britain. Her nursing and naval contacts helped her find a Nursing Officer in the Queen Alexandra's Royal Naval Nursing Service stationed at the naval base hospital, who was a very experienced midwife and she figured that the combination of this Nursing Officer and one of the doctors at the hospital, whom she knew had had long experience in a civilian general practice before joining the Navy, should between them be able to see her and the baby through the birth. She reminded herself that she was in excellent health, it would be her third birth and there was no reason to expect complications. So she wasn't too worried, and this proved justified when, with the doctor and Nursing Officer in attendance, she delivered a healthy full term baby boy at the naval base hospital. They named him Roger.

To help her after the birth, Mary had arranged to employ an Egyptian nurse who had worked for European families, spoke good English and had long experience in looking after new mothers and newborn babies. She would join the household when Mary came home from the hospital with the baby and stay there for several weeks.

Mary had decided against having any of the naval hospital doctors circumcise her baby, as she had not established to her satisfaction that any of them had the same skill and experience with the operation as the surgeon who had circumcised John and she didn't want to run any unnecessary surgical risks, or indeed any risk of Roger having anything less than a cosmetically perfect circumcision. On the other hand she was uneasily aware that the family might not return to Britain before Roger was a toddler and she didn't want him to undergo circumcision at an age when it would be a frightening ordeal for him. Every time she bathed Roger or changed his nappy she was reminded of the dilemma facing her.

It was the nurse she was employing who pointed the way to a solution. The nurse had worked in Alexandria for several of the very wealthy Jewish families who lived there and had assisted at the ritual circumcisions of their sons held on the eighth day after birth. The ritual circumcision or bris was performed by a religious official called a mohel who had undergone rigorous training in doing circumcisions. Some of the mohelim were qualified doctors who combined a regular medical practice with officiating at brisses. The nurse told Mary that the standard of surgery the mohelim practised was very high. Two doctors of European origin and training were mohelim and both of them accepted non-Jewish cases. She had assisted both at brisses and, although neither she nor her husband was Jewish, she had had her own son circumcised by one of them and he had also circumcised her nephew. Her son was now two years old and her nephew a year old and if Mary wished, she could bring them to Mary's house so that she could see for herself how well the surgery had been performed. When she saw the two little boys on the following day Mary was impressed with the mohel's craftsmanship. She made further inquiries of two British mothers for whom the nurse had worked and who, although not Jewish, had had their sons circumcised by the mohel and she also spoke to two local doctors who had attended the mothers when the babies were born. All recommended him.

After talking to her husband she asked the nurse to contact the mohel.

The nurse arranged for the mohel to call at the house to see Mary and her husband. There were considerable language difficulties but the nurse managed to interpret and also to translate the several letters of reference that the mohel brought with him. A fee was settled – a very reasonable one in Mary's view – and the operation set for the following day. As the baby was not to be fed after midnight because of the risk of his vomiting and choking during the operation, it was arranged that he would come to Mary's house early the next morning. Mary thought to herself – but did not say to her husband – that, although she was fully satisfied as to the mohel's competence, this circumcision might be a bit bizarre compared with the others she had witnessed in England.

Mary awaited the mohel's arrival the following morning with a mother's natural trepidation; it was her baby who was to be operated on and, although she was satisfied the procedure had long term benefits for him, it was going to be very painful for him. After the mohel arrived he made his preparations and Mary, who watched him like a hawk, was impressed by his scrupulous standards of cleanliness of instruments and person which matched those found in any British hospital.

When all was ready Mary removed Roger's nappy and handed him to the nurse who was seated on a chair and laid him on her lap. She held him in such a way that he could not move at all. The restraint irked him and he began to cry almost immediately. Mary placed a sugar cube, which had been wrapped in gauze by the mohel and dipped in brandy, between the baby's lips to give him something to suck on and comfort him. The mohel applied an antiseptic to the penis. Roger's crying increased as the mohel tried to ease his foreskin back and, failing to retract it, used a probe to separate the foreskin from the underlying glans, which made Roger scream. Having broken down the adhesions between the glans and the foreskin, the mohel was able to retract the foreskin and he applied more antiseptic before moving the foreskin back so that it again covered the glans. He then massaged the tiny penis to a slight erection. Picking up a small flat metal shield with a slit in it he pulled Roger's foreskin through the slit and adjusted the angle of the shield to lie parallel with the base of the baby's glans. Working with great speed and dexterity, he took up a small knife sharpened on both edges and, using the top surface of the shield as a guide, he sliced through Roger's foreskin. Then, putting down the shield, he trimmed away the remains of the inner surface of the foreskin covering the glans so the whole of the glans was laid bare. Roger's cries were now weaker but his little face was purple and contorted with pain. The mohel aligned the cut surfaces of the foreskin and after applying more antiseptic and some Vaseline, he bandaged Roger's penis.

Mary had watched intently. The whole operation had been much quicker than those in British hospitals and although Roger had screamed piercingly, she comforted herself with the thought that it was no more painful and the whole procedure of much shorter duration than if he had had the operation in a hospital in Britain. Still, she felt shaky, and asked the nurse to bring Roger to her in her bedroom as quickly as possible so that she could give him the comfort of being fed. She thanked the mohel before following the nurse into her bedroom. Roger's mouth tightened round her nipple and he sucked greedily as she fed him, leaving the nurse to help the mohel pack his instruments and supplies. Roger fell into a rather fitful sleep immediately he had had his fill and stopped sucking.

The mohel came to change the dressing the following morning and Mary was pleased to be able to confirm the impression she had received while watching the surgery that it had been very well performed. When paying him Mary thanked him again, less hurriedly than on the previous day, and told him how pleased she was with the result. Roger made an uneventful recovery and Mary was delighted with the neat appearance of his penis with its bare glans. His circumcision was as cosmetically perfect as John's and she was greatly relieved that he was safely through the ordeal.

Later Mary wrote to the mohel to thank him for his services

and with a view to helping him to extend his practice among British families she enclosed a testimonial letter reading –

"To whom it may concern:
The above-named physician and mohel performed a circumcision on my 3 week old son as a non-religious case.
I am a British qualified nurse with extensive experience as an operating theatre sister and I have assisted at many circumcisions in British hospitals. My son's circumcision was most carefully and skilfully performed in my presence with all aseptic precautions, healing being uneventful and rapid. In my professional opinion, the circumcision removed the optimum amount of foreskin and the result is surgically and cosmetically excellent.
The above-named was recommended to me by Mrs. Nadia Nasser who has provided post-partum nursing care for many other expatriate families and whose own son and nephew had been circumcised, also as non-religious cases, by the above-named.
I am more than happy to recommend the above-named and would be pleased to discuss my recommendation with any mother wishing to have her son circumcised."

Before Roger's birth Kate had asked her mother to let her see her new brother's penis before and after his circumcision. Before the circumcision, Mary had made sure that Kate had the opportunity of seeing Roger's penis with its foreskin still intact by letting her help bathe him several times. Mary showed Kate that his foreskin was not freely movable and explained that it was still bonded to the glans. Mary waited until Roger's circumcision had healed sufficiently for him to be bathed normally before letting Kate assist in bathing him again. She told her mother that she was glad that both her brothers now had nice looking penises. She said she thought that both Roger and Joan's baby looked much better circumcised than uncircumcised. Before the operation, she said, their penises "looked a little bit like worms."

Chapter 2

Nursing School

Kate and her family returned to the austerity and gloom of post-war Britain when her father left the Navy. Kate and her brothers were bright youngsters who all did well in school and her parents hoped that she would go to university to study medicine, but when the time came for her to decide what she wanted to do Kate told her parents that, even though her exam results qualified her for entrance to medical school, she didn't want to become a doctor, saying that it was a long and expensive grind and if she married and had children she would prefer to be at home with them and did not want then to regret the time and money spent on a qualification she wasn't using. "No," she said, "I'd rather do what you did, Mum, and go into nursing. Not to empty bedpans but to be, like you were before I was born, at the sharp end, a surgical nurse and hopefully one day, like you, a theatre sister."

So Kate went into nursing school at the Royal Infirmary, the large teaching hospital attached to the university in her home town. She continued to live at home although most of her fellow students, a lively bunch of girls, lived in the nurses' home. An attractive girl, Kate was rather quiet, shy and introspective – less outgoing than most of her fellow student nurses who were making the most of their new found opportunities to meet young men in the hospital and university.

Although Kate didn't live in the nurses' home she was frequently invited by her fellow first year students to visit them there. Sometimes she would visit a friend in the room she occupied and there might be a get-together of several students in the room, but if the gathering got too big for the room, the group would move to the student nurses' common room where they would mingle with more senior nursing students.

In the common room discussions were frequent and spontaneous. There was no formality. A discussion might be confined to a small group or, depending on the topic, become more general. Where the subject was of general interest keen debate sometimes ensued and if the topic was a technical one and some participants were particularly knowledgeable, it might evolve into an informal mini-seminar. A favourite topic was sex and Kate, being straight out of a girls' school and by nature quite reserved, was surprised by the frankness of speech and lack of inhibition - particularly the lack of reticence when describing personal experiences and the lessons to be drawn from them. At first she was mildly embarrassed but before long she realized how much she was enjoying what she was hearing - and how much she was learning from it, too. She was beginning her sexual awakening.

The subjects discussed didn't follow any agenda and the discussions were impromptu and unstructured. Someone would mention something and points of view and relevant experiences came tumbling out and if the topic struck a chord with several of those present, there would be extended discussion, sometimes a lengthy one. Much depended on how many students were present and who they were. Looking back on discussions they had heard in the common room, Kate and Judith, both first year students, privately labelled these informal meetings of nursing students "The Institute of Advanced Sexology." Judith and Kate had been attracted to each other as friends from their first meeting as new students at the nursing school; they were both highly intelligent and sexually inexperienced, fresh from all girls' schools. Both found the discussions in the common room fascinating and instructive.

Kate got into the habit of writing notes during each discussion which interested her, recording the things said which she thought worth remembering and editing them later. She kept the notes in a binder and as time went by and she became more knowledgeable herself, she added her own thoughts which she had been too diffident or shy to express in the common room or had come to her as she wrote the notes. She hid the binder in her bedroom at home in a place where she thought it would be safe from the eyes of her brothers. Her notes recorded discussions on a wide variety of medical and nursing subjects as well as such topics as contraception, safe periods, at what point in a relationship a girl should allow what intimacies, what made a boy attractive to a girl, what made a girl attractive to a boy, making one's career compatible with motherhood, how many children to have and at what ages, sexual techniques, first intercourse and defloration, oral lovemaking and many other topics of interest to a group of young adult females with a healthy interest in sex.

Kate's notes of one informal common room debate, which she found particularly interesting and well argued by the participating nursing students and several graduate nurses who were by chance visiting the common room, read –

"Circumcision

Ranged from boyfriends, fiancés and husbands to babies. Vigorous debate. Distaff replay of English Civil War between cavaliers on the one side and roundheads on the other. Best argued debate yet. Quite heated at times.

The discussion was sparked by Janet who made a casual comment about the whole male community being divided into those who had been circumcised and those who had not. She thought the designation of roundhead and cavalier for the two groups was a witty one. Women should welcome the diversity as it gave us a choice.

The debate began when Elizabeth commented that she enjoyed the excitement of seeing her fiancé's foreskin retracting to reveal his glans. When questioned about hygiene, she said she saw no problem because any male worth marrying or even dating would keep himself clean "down there" anyway. She thought her fiancé's "hooded wonder" looked nice and he had good lasting qualities. If she had a son she would keep him intact.

Margaret disagreed totally. To her, as a nurse, health and hygiene were paramount, and this meant universal routine infant circumcision. Jewish women had a much lower incidence of cancer of the cervix than women of races whose males were not circumcised. The only women with better immunity from cancer of the cervix were nuns and (amid laughter) "their immunity doesn't help us." The glans not protected, and so not constricted, by a foreskin developed as a larger glans, which had the effect of increasing the friction between the penis and the vaginal wall, and it also developed a tougher and less sensitive surface, which helped to delay the owner's orgasm; furthermore, throughout intercourse, the glans of a circumcised penis was in full contact with the vaginal wall and this gave a woman more stimulation than an uncircumcised penis where the glans tended to be covered by the foreskin on outward strokes of the penis. All these three factors associated with circumcision were beneficial in assisting the woman to attain orgasm. Early circumcision totally eliminated the possibility of cancer of the penis. A neatly circumcised penis looked much better than one with a foreskin and was much more appealing, hygienically and aesthetically, particularly to a woman who enjoyed performing fellatio on her man. Circumcision was a safe, trivial procedure in a newborn and if Americans, Canadians and Australians continued to treat it as a routine procedure for most newborn boys, why shouldn't the National Health Service ("NHS") allow it on a mother's request? The student nurses of our generation were lucky that our future husbands had been born before the NHS had effectively banned circumcision; the next generation would be less fortunate. She herself was lucky – her fiancé had been circumcised soon after his birth, very neatly too. When she had a baby boy he was definitely going to be done.

Someone asked Judith what she, being Jewish, thought. She said she was fortunate – she would never have to make a choice about circumcision. When she married it would be to another

Jew and he would have been circumcised. When she had a son he would in accordance with Jewish law be circumcised on the 8th day after his birth. So no choice, no problem, for her either as wife or mother. But she had nursed gentile boys and men who had not been circumcised and, as a nurse, she preferred circumcision for its better hygiene; also, to be frank, she did not like the appearance of an uncircumcised penis. Even if she wasn't Jewish she would want any husband or son of hers to be circumcised for health and aesthetic reasons.

Shirley argued that the only people entitled to venture an opinion on whether women found sexual intercourse or fellatio more satisfactory with a circumcised or an uncircumcised lover were women who had had experience with several men of both varieties, and preferably with men before and after they'd been circumcised. She admitted that this was a tall order but necessary if any conclusions were to have scientific credibility. When asked, she said she was prepared to organise a research programme if enough of those present would volunteer for "fieldwork" as she delicately put it. (Raucous applause).

Catherine agreed with every point made by Margaret. Circumcision had never been as common in Britain as it had become in the USA and Canada, but when she was in maternity she found that many of the new mums had circumcised husbands, were used to circumcision and wanted their sons circumcised. They were being told that circumcision wasn't available. That was bad, but, worse than that, they were being fobbed off - and, in her view, actually lied to - by being told that circumcision was not only unnecessary and barbaric but carried a substantial (but unquantified) risk of injury or even death. She had read that when a baby boy was born in pre-NHS days it was the mother, not the father, who usually made the decision for or against circumcision, and that in deciding the mother tended to rely on the advice of her own mother. She thought it a bit odd that the status of a man's penis might ultimately depend on his maternal grandmother's whim. Her boyfriend and her brother had been circumcised. She was satisfied that a circumcised penis was easier to keep clean and virtually "maintenance free" and she really liked the neat appearance a properly performed circumcision gave. Her first two boyfriends had been uncircumcised and she was very happy that her present one had had the "snip" – no problem with premature ejaculation which had afflicted one of her other boyfriends.

Stephanie also agreed wholeheartedly with Margaret. When on maternity she had encountered the same situation as Catherine and, like her, her conscience had been troubled by what hospital policy required her to tell new mums wanting their sons circumcised. She had told the mums that she was too junior to give an answer and suggested they ask old Sister "Starchy" on the theory that as Sister S had never had intimate connection with any penis, snipped or unsnipped, she should at least be able to give objective advice. (Much laughter - Sister S being regarded by the student body as the archetypal ancient spinster nursing sister as well as a self-appointed guardian of the virginity of students).

Joanna, who had been evacuated to USA during the war and lived there until returning to Britain to go to the nursing school, commented that one argument advanced by the anti-circumcision faction was surgical risk and it had been said that before the NHS effectively abolished circumcision on demand an average of 16 boys a year died in Britain from circumcision "accidents". If this figure was true, it was an appalling indictment of British medical competence. In the USA, by comparison, such deaths were extremely rare although the US population was 4 times that of Britain and 80-90% of US baby boys were routinely circumcised in hospitals before discharge after birth. Why was circumcision so much safer in the USA than in Britain? Could it be simply that the operation done routinely was safer because those operating were more experienced in doing circumcisions? She too preferred a circumcised penis and any son of hers would be circumcised, but she would choose a Jewish doctor or someone she knew to be expert at circumcision.

There was one aspect of circumcision which troubled Deborah and that was the lack of pain relief at circumcisions of newborns and babies up to several months of age. It was nonsense to say that their nervous systems were insufficiently developed to register pain – the piercing screams and contorted faces they had all heard and seen belied that. She was aware of the risks involved in giving general anaesthetics to young babies but some form of local anaesthesia should be possible. She took no comfort in the argument that the pain suffered by a baby being circumcised was outweighed by the long term benefits of the operation – try telling that one to the baby, she said. Circumcisions performed by mohels were far quicker than those done by hospital staff and she thought Jewish babies benefited from this fact. Despite her reservations about pain relief, if she had a son he would be circumcised, preferably by a mohel or a Jewish doctor, but she would make sure that he received some form of pain relief.

During the discussion, several girls said that they were happy with their boyfriends' or fiancés' penises, some being circumcised and some not. (I think loyalty to the boyfriend rather than scientific objectivity inspired these comments and it may be that these girls had only had experience of one kind of penis.) Several of those present said whether they would or would not have their sons circumcised. One girl said she would never marry or have intercourse with an uncircumcised man. Several were in principle opposed to any surgery unless it was necessary on the grounds that all surgery imported some risk however small. Fellatio was mentioned and it seemed that some girls who would have full intercourse with an uncircumcised man would not fellate him. (Odd, I thought.)

Catherine (again) said that her eldest sister qualified in nursing and had strong views on circumcision. She had left nursing when she married just before the inception of the NHS. Later when she gave birth to a baby boy she had asked for him to be circumcised before she left the hospital where he was born. She was told that circumcision was no longer available unless medically necessary. She was outraged and said "No self-respecting nurse ever left hospital with an uncircumcised son!" The baby was circumcised privately. Her sister had since wondered what would have happened if she had gone on strike and refused to leave the hospital until her baby had been circumcised.

Joanna (again) accepted that many foreskins were unretractable or not easily retractable until their owners were 3-5 years old and this was used as an argument against early circumcisions. But what about the 10% or so whose foreskins never became retractable? She knew of cases of adult males who could not retract. Older infants and adults needed general anaesthesia and more complicated surgery with the associated risks, much higher costs and inconvenience and embarrassment to the patient. She wondered whether economic analysis would not justify the NHS adopting the US practice of routine infant circumcision.

Stephanie (again) pointed out that NHS policy had not permeated Buckingham Palace. It was well known that Prince Charles, born after the NHS had been established, was circumcised as a baby following the tradition established by Queen Victoria that all royal princes were circumcised by a Jewish mohel.

A visiting graduate of the nursing school said she understood that about 25% of British males were circumcised in pre-NHS days. In the course of their work, nurses became aware of the results of a lack of penile hygiene, and she suspected that the percentage of the sons of nurses who were circumcised was a good deal higher than in the population at large. She had worked in the sanatoriums of two leading boys' public schools and she had the impression that at one school about two-thirds of the boys had been circumcised and at the other, the more famous of the two, at least 80%, perhaps even 90%, had been done. These were children of wealthy families to whom the best medical care and advice were available. This indicated to her that the best medical practice obviously favoured routine infant circumcision on the US pattern. The effect of the NHS ban on circumcision on request was to the disadvantage of parents who couldn't afford to go private. Was this in accordance with the ideals of those who had campaigned for a state medical service to bring high quality medical care to all irrespective of their means? She thought not.

Jenny asked how one would go about asking a boyfriend whom one fancied, but had not yet "had intimate relations with" (as she put it), whether he was circumcised. "That's a hot potato" was one view, but Trish, a senior student, was scathing – "Ask him, of course. If you're lucky he'll tell you he doesn't know and ask if you would be kind enough to give him a professional opinion." Others tried to give more helpful advice. Jenny bravely pressed on to a second question and asked how one would ask an uncircumcised man that one wanted to marry if he would be prepared to undergo circumcision before marriage. Trish jumped in again and said that if he loved Jenny enough to want to marry her surely he would be prepared to sacrifice a little scrap of useless tissue, but Jenny should make it clear that she didn't expect him to show her love for her to the extent of forgoing an anaesthetic. Again, others dealt with her question and gave more sympathetic advice.

It was getting late and discussion came to a close when, amid laughter, someone proposed a two part vote –

-that this House favours circumcised boyfriends and husbands, and

-that this House favours the routine circumcision of all sons of this House soon after birth.

The discussion was mostly serious but well leavened with humour and proved, if it needed to be proved, that circumcision is a controversial topic among us students. The participants knew what they were talking about. For obvious reasons circumcision is a subject which interests young adults, but what surprised me was the passion engendered on both sides of the debate – it was far and away the best and most lively common room discussion I had attended yet, being well argued pro and con circumcision.

Personally I agreed with everything that Margaret had said – it was very much the line preached by Mum who is very much in favour of routine circumcision and arranged for both my brothers to be circumcised as newborns. If Mum hadn't already convinced me – and she had – that discussion would have convinced me. I know that I want my husband and any son(s) of mine to be circumcised."

Kate found the nursing school stimulating – the lecturers were enthusiastic, interesting and well-prepared, and she enjoyed being rotated from department to department in the hospital, as it gave her the widest possible training and experience and the opportunity to decide what field of nursing interested her the most. She enjoyed the maternity department where cases had an overwhelming incidence of happy outcomes and found some departments stimulating and others depressing. Her early ambition to follow her mother into operating theatre work was reinforced when she first watched the surgeons at work and later was assigned junior roles in the theatres.

While Kate took full advantage of the opportunities for forming friendships with her fellow students in the nursing school she also enjoyed the companionship of the nurses she worked with in the Royal Infirmary. As she was rotated for training and work experience through various departments she found herself temporarily attached as a student to teams of nurses staffing the departments and wards and got to know a wide cross-section of the nursing staff while working alongside them. A lot of her training was "on the job" - learning from more experienced colleagues as they went about their duties and asking questions. The nurses worked in shifts and whenever possible took their breaks for coffee, lunch, tea or supper together in small groups. The range of ages was considerable and, because of the depth of experience of her senior colleagues, Kate found the conversations during breaks, and particularly the longer lunch and supper breaks, could be most interesting and enlightening, both professionally and personally.

Not long after the debate on circumcision in the student nurses' common room Kate spent a supper break in the company of three nurses she was working with in the maternity wing. All were in their thirties, two being married and one single, and the same topic arose but this time it was discussed by an older group than the common room participants and the emphasis was on personal experience. The trio were close personal friends as well as colleagues and, despite Kate's presence, were quite uninhibited in comparing their experiences as were three other nurses who joined them later. Kate was fascinated and after she got home she made a note recording the discussion which she filed with her note of the common room debate. It read as follows-

"Circumcision revisited – a senior review
Participants: Pauline (married, one son), Patricia (twice married, no child) and Marianne (never married, no child), all Mat. Wg. nurses in 30s.

Performance in bed of their partners, past and present, circumcised and uncircumcised, compared (rather unscientifically as loyalty and strength of attachment would have precluded objective assessments of performance!)

Joined later by Eileen (40, widow, one son, op. theatre sister) and Megan and Marjorie (both Mat. Wg. nurses in their 50s, married, each with several children).

Pauline's husband had suffered an injury to his penis after they married (here Patricia, Marianne and I giggled, driving an indignant Pauline to deny that she had any part in his accident, which resulted from an unfortunate encounter with a zip-fastener). As his foreskin had been torn, treatment for the injury was a circumcision. She thought that the circumcision had enhanced his qualities as a lover – he seemed to last longer before climaxing and that had helped her to attain orgasm more frequently post-op than pre-op – but there were improvements also in hygiene and appearance. Now he had a penis which was easier to keep clean. Gone was the elephant trunk like foreskin which had previously spoiled the pleasure she would otherwise have had in fellating him – something, however, she had nevertheless done for his sake even though she did not enjoy retracting his foreskin and taking into her mouth a penis head which lived in a perpetually moist environment under its hood. Its new look and flavour were so much better, and so was its appearance of being always ready for action. She much preferred it post-op. Actually, from her earliest days of training as a nurse she had liked the appearance of a circumcised organ better and on her wedding night when she had at last been able to satisfy her curiosity about her groom's status by actual inspection she had been mildly disappointed to find him intact. When (in pre-NHS days) they had a baby son she made sure he was among the 20% or so, mostly middle-class, male infants circumcised before they left the hospital. Her husband was in total agreement and in arranging her baby's circumcision, she received good support from the ward staff, several of whom told her that they had had their own sons done or planned to do so if they ever had boy babies. She had herself assisted the registrar who circumcised her baby at several circumcisions while she had been working in the maternity dept before her baby's birth, knew him to be particularly competent and she had asked him to perform the op himself. He had done an excellent job on her son. A nurse, who was a personal friend and long time colleague of Pauline's, assisted the registrar at the circumcision. She collected Pauline's baby from her for his circumcision and later when she returned him to her after his short absence from the ward told her that when she had a little boy of her own she hoped that his circumcision would be as skilfully performed and as neat as Pauline's baby's. Pauline said she was very happy that both her husband and her son had been circumcised: if she had had another son he would have been done, too – preferably by the same registrar.

Patricia said that the first man she had been intimate with had not been circumcised and she had been "absolutely fascinated" by the visually dramatic process of his erection – how his penis became larger and larger and how as it grew the foreskin retracted itself to reveal the glans until she was confronted by what appeared to her as a teenager to be a massive throbbing truncheon with a large acorn shaped head. Her own primary sexual organs were all within her body concealed from view and she found the sheer blatancy of the contrast awesome.

Maybe it was vanity on her part but as a woman the thought that, even without her touching him, her mere proximity to a man could set in motion a process by which a small soft sausage-like structure with its end covered in skin could so dramatically enlarge itself, divest itself of the skin covering and metamorphose into a rampant battering ram specifically designed for the purpose of entering her vagina thrilled her. Later she had found that she experienced great pleasure in taking his flaccid penis into her hand and gently pulling the fleshy foreskin back to reveal the pink glans it concealed. She admitted that she was addicted to intact penises. Her first lover had been fastidious about cleanliness and she never had any problem in fellating him, only pleasure. Vaginal intercourse had been very satisfying and he could control the timing of his orgasm so that she could be sure of attaining her climax.

Patricia's second lover whom she had married had been circumcised. She said she understood the hygienic advantages of a circumcised penis with its permanently bared head and could appreciate that it appealed aesthetically to others, even if she herself preferred the appearance of an intact penis. He gave her satisfactory vaginal intercourse and she had enjoyed fellating him. Seeing his penis become larger during erection gave her pleasure, but she missed the drama of a foreskin retracting to show her an engorged glans. A circumcised penis simply could not react in such a visually dramatic way as an intact penis and consequently, other things being equal, making love with a circumcised man was not as satisfying for her as with an uncircumcised man. But their ultimate divorce stemmed from other problems.

Patricia's present husband had not been circumcised. She thought his performance in bed was as good or better than his two predecessors, and she thoroughly enjoyed vaginal intercourse and fellating him. She said that if they had a son, she would be in a "real quandary" over circumcision. Although as a woman, her own sexual preference was for an uncircumcised lover, she admitted that as a nurse she found the health and hygiene arguments in favour of circumcision "rather uncomfortably compelling." Replying to Pauline's question, she said that if she decided in favour of circumcising a son it would be conditional on her husband agreeing to it and in seeking his concurrence she would make it very clear to him that the circumcision was for reasons of health and hygiene and that for lovemaking she personally much preferred an uncircumcised penis like his.

Marianne, never having married, had no compromises to make out of loyalty to a spouse. At 30, younger than the other two. Very forthright views. She too had experience of both circumcised and intact lovers and, other things being equal, much preferred the shorn variety. She thought the hooded kind looked "ugly, wrinkled and plain untidy." When a penis had been circumcised properly - and she laid great emphasis on the skill and competence of the operator – it was more hygienic, looked better and, to her this was important, appeared ready to make love to her even when it wasn't erect. Whether as a nurse or bed mate she didn't like an uncircumcised penis. She didn't like having to retract something which she thought shouldn't be there anyway. However carefully and frequently the owner washed himself, the glans underneath would be moist, possibly even slimy, and a prepuce was an ideal hiding place for debris. Although Marianne enjoyed fellating a man who had had a full circumcision with the glans permanently laid bare, she had found going down on intact men much less pleasant and on occasion downright unthinkable. She was convinced that a circumcised penis had a less sensitive head and so tended to last longer before reaching orgasm and the longer a man lasted the more likely it was that the woman would herself attain a satisfactory climax. She was "pretty sure" that the head of a penis circumcised in infancy tended to be larger than that of an intact organ. During intercourse both the extra size of the head and the fact that there was no foreskin to interpose itself between the rim of the head and the vagina increased the friction the penis exerted on the vaginal wall resulting in more sexual stimulation during intercourse. For all these reasons she would much prefer to marry a circumcised man, but if she fell in love with a man who hadn't been done she would marry him although she wouldn't promise not to try to persuade him to have the snip before, or even after, she got him to the altar. Besides, wouldn't it be great to be able to boast to her closest friends that she had a husband who had proved his love for her by being circumcised at her request? (Marianne is charming as well as extremely good looking and elegant and when – not if – she marries I am prepared to bet that any unneeded tissue will have been charmed away from her fiancé's private parts before their wedding day!)

If Marianne has a baby boy she will have him circumcised and, because of the NHS ban, she says she will go private and have it done by a mohel or a Jewish doctor as this has advantages over a run of the mill hospital circumcision in guaranteeing a proper circumcision with a completely uncovered glans and less suffering for her son as it will be quicker and more competently performed. In answer to Patricia, she agreed that circumcision was painful but the pain was of short duration and the benefits lifelong. Furthermore, many boys had tight foreskins which ultimately needed retraction or circumcision. Retraction, whether done by the mother or a doctor, was usually also painful, although admittedly not nearly as painful as an un-anesthetised circumcision, and needed to be repeated regularly until the foreskin was freed enough to allow easy retraction. Mothers were often reluctant to attempt retraction or, because they knew it hurt their sons, to repeat the treatment, yet repetition was necessary for success. Circumcision could be a major ordeal for a toddler as it meant hospitalisation. She favoured routine infant circumcision on the US model.

Eileen, who had sat down to join us while Pauline was speaking, is a friend of my mother and had worked with her in surgery pre-war. Very nice, one super lady. I've known her all my life and am very fond of her. Her husband, a doctor, was killed during the war while serving in the RN and she came back into nursing to augment her tiny war widow's pension and help support herself and her son. When she saw me in the group she gave me a great beaming smile and came over to sit next to me saying, "Welcome to the baby shop, Kate!" After Marianne had made her comments, Eileen said that she agreed with everything Marianne had said. On her wedding night she had been relieved to see that her husband had been circumcised as she preferred it for hygienic reasons and thought it looked better. During their honeymoon she had told him that if they ever had a son she would want him circumcised like him. When her son was born she would have had him circumcised anyway because of her belief in the health and appearance benefits, but as he was born after his father's death she had an additional, very personal motive for wanting him to be like his father, so her baby's circumcision was a very emotional event for her. She had asked a Jewish doctor who was a friend of her husband and herself to perform the circumcision and it had been done in her house while she held her son on her lap. Before the circumcision, while bathing the baby, she had managed gradually "with diligence and patience" to free his foreskin so that by the time of the op it was retractable which would make the op quicker and easier on the baby than if the doctor had first to break down the adhesions between the glans and foreskin. As an analgesic she had given the baby a sugar cube soused in brandy which had belonged to her husband to suck on as she prepped him pre-op and a second one just before the op, but while being circumcised he had screamed as all babies do and continued to do so until she put him to her breast as soon as the op was over and he had been bandaged. Although she knew it would be an ordeal, Eileen had held him for his circumcision because she hoped it would comfort him but she had found his distress heartrending – "Even worse than when I was holding some other mother's baby during his circumcision, but it was my decision to circumcise my son and I owed it to him to support him and, so far as I could, share his pain." Turning to me, she said how lucky she was to have my mother as a friend. They had known each other as theatre nurses and Mum had been very supportive of her after her husband was killed. She had asked Mum to be with her during her little son's circumcision to give her "the courage and resolve I knew I would need and in case I found at the last moment I couldn't face up to holding my baby during his op" and Mum had helped to prep the baby and with his aftercare, including making daily visits to change the dressings. *"Your mother was an absolute brick then and on many other occasions before and since. A wonderful friend to me."* Surgically and cosmetically the result was perfect and the wound had healed in less than a week. After that whenever she bathed or changed him she felt a sense of pleasure at the neat appearance.

While Marianne was making her contribution to the discussion, two other nurses had joined the group and listened with interest. They were older, both in their fifties, married and each with several children.

Megan said that when she joined the hospital as a trainee some of the sister tutors had been nursing since long before the first world war and it had been interesting to hear their perspectives on how medicine and nursing had changed during their working lifetimes. She remembered one of her tutors in midwifery saying that when she started maternity nursing about 50% of baby boys were circumcised and that among the sons of very well off parents anything up to 85% were done. Megan said she understood that circumcision was not practised in England except as a Jewish ritual until Queen Victoria's reign and believed that once it became known that Victoria had had her own sons circumcised it became fashionable among upper class families and later gradually spread to the middle class, but working class parents had not taken to it with the same enthusiasm, perhaps deterred by the doctor's fee for the extra service. But the percentages quoted by her tutor struck Megan as very high. Be that as it may, circumcision was not a new phenomenon, nor was it a new controversy as she remembered doctors and nurses arguing the pros and cons throughout her own career and this discussion showed it had not been resolved yet, and perhaps never would be.

Marianne asked Megan whether in Victorian times the principal reason for circumcision becoming popular was not so much improved hygiene and health but because it was believed *that it would prevent boys masturbating. Megan said that circumcision had certainly been propagated as a treatment to prevent masturbation by eliminating the possibility of irritating material being retained under the prepuce and so get rid of what was then believed to be the cause of masturbation, but she laughed as she said she couldn't believe that the theory could have held water for long as anyone who had cared for children knew that all boys masturbated, the ones who had been circumcised at least as enthusiastically as the ones left intact.*

When Megan's own three sons had been born at home in the 1920s, her family doctor had asked her after each birth whether she wanted her baby circumcised and each time she had said no. If she had requested a circumcision it would have been done in her own home by the family doctor with the midwife or district nurse holding the baby on her lap. Although she had qualified as a nurse before marrying and was familiar with circumcision, she had decided against it for her own sons because her husband was uncircumcised and had had no problems and she considered that she would be able to take care of any possible tight foreskin problems when bathing her sons. Except for rare cases of phimosis, she understood that most tight foreskin problems disappeared of their own accord as boys grew up and discovered the pleasure they felt when they manipulated their penises. In fact one of her sons did have a non-retractable foreskin but she had been able over a period to ease it back gently and progressively while bathing him. It had required patience but by the time he was ready for school the problem had been resolved and he had never complained that she had hurt him.

Marjorie said that her husband had not been circumcised and she had not had either of her sons circumcised for much the same reasons as Megan, adding that she was against unnecessary surgery. Her older son was married. She got on very well with her daughter-in-law who came from a family in which circumcision was the norm and when she became pregnant she had talked to Marjorie about circumcision if the baby she was carrying was a boy. Marjorie had told her she thought it was generally unnecessary unless a boy had a genuine phimosis. That was rare and could not be diagnosed until the age of 5 at earliest. Her daughter-in-law said that all three of her brothers had been circumcised as newborns and she had grown up believing that it was normal for baby boys to be circumcised. It was not until she married that she had realized that circumcision wasn't always performed or necessary. Her own mother had advised her to have her baby circumcised if a boy. She said her husband, Marjorie's son, was ambivalent saying that he had had no problems but that it was a trivial operation in a newborn and he would support her in whatever decision she made. Patricia asked Marjorie whether she had had a grandson and if so had he been circumcised. Marjorie laughed and said that the baby hadn't yet been born and that her daughter-in-law was still between a rock and a hard place, her mother and Marjorie, but she had made up her mind to tell her daughter-in-law the next time she came to see her that if she would feel more comfortable with a baby who had been circumcised she should go ahead and get it done. "After all, I won't love him any less! I'll keep you posted on the outcome."

The others now turned to me, much junior to any of them and the only one who hadn't spoken. What did I think? I started by admitting that, although I had never been intimate with a man and was therefore the least qualified of any present to make any judgment on circumcision, I actually held very strong views, theoretical rather than practical though they might be. I had been brought up by a mother who had been a theatre sister and strongly in favour of all baby boys being circumcised. (Here Eileen nodded in support.) I had grown up with two circumcised brothers and, although I knew that not all boys were circumcised, circumcision was the norm so far as I was concerned before I started nurse training. In the hospital I had had to look after males of all ages, some of them circumcised, but the great majority not. I had assisted at several circumcisions, mostly babies but a few older boys and one adolescent. I was not in a position to compare the performance of shorn and unshorn penises but I had seen enough of each type under hospital conditions to convince me of the hygienic and aesthetic advantages of circumcision. In saying this I said I certainly didn't want the others there to think I was arrogant or dogmatic, but from what I had seen and read so far I thought my mother was right and that circumcision is advantageous. I hoped that if I married I would have a circumcised husband and if I had a son I would have him circumcised, preferably by a mohel or a Jewish doctor. I said I thought my views came close to Marianne's and Eileen's.

Marianne said that if everyone didn't think we had flogged circumcision to death there was something more she wanted to say before the supper break ended. She, Eileen and Kate thought that all males ought to be circumcised and, although Pauline hadn't actually said so, she presumed that Pauline did, too. (Pauline nodded.) Marianne said she was bothered by the fact that almost all infant circumcisions up to about the age of 4 months were done without anaesthesia. She had started nursing before the NHS had vetoed non-therapeutic circumcisions and had held too many squirming, screaming babies undergoing circumcision without an anaesthetic to swallow the oft peddled line that babies of that age don't feel pain and were merely registering an objection to being restrained while the op was done. "That is bollocks," she said, "of course they feel pain. We've all held babies being circumcised and" (amid nods of agreement) "we know they feel great pain." She certainly wouldn't like to have that kind of surgery performed on her without an anaesthetic. She had assisted at several Jewish ritual circumcisions on week old babies as well as many non-ritual circumcisions and was in a position to compare them. The Jewish bris was performed by a specialist, the mohel, who might or might not be a doctor, but in either case had undergone a rigorous course of training in performing this one operation using a technique which ensured that exactly the right amount of tissue was removed so that the glans was permanently and completely bared and a good surgical and cosmetic result achieved. The precision of the surgery was impressive but so was the speed at which the mohel worked. Unlike hospital *surgeons the mohel always operated under the close scrutiny of the baby's parents and relatives and friends who themselves were familiar with the technique and expected a cosmetically perfect operation completed within two or three minutes and the mohel was aware that each time he operated his future reputation depended on the onlookers' judgement. The baby was sedated before and during the operation by being given wine or brandy to dull the pain. The speed of the Jewish procedure and the sedation given contrasted with the ten or twenty minutes or so which a surgeon or general practitioner took to operate on a (normally) fully conscious and un-sedated baby with a result which usually fell short of the standard achieved by a mohel. Furthermore, the Jewish baby was not operated on in the isolation of a hospital treatment room but surrounded by his parents and close family, which might give him some psychological support, and could be put to his mother's breast to be fed immediately after his ordeal. Marianne's experience had led her to believe that Jewish babies ritually circumcised were less traumatised than boys non-ritually circumcised. "If I'm ever lucky enough to marry and have a baby and it's a boy I will want him to be circumcised for all the hygienic, health and, yes, sexual advantages which I believe will accrue to him and any future wife of his as well as the aesthetic benefits. I think that Jewish ritual circumcisions are more skilfully performed than most hospital ones. They're certainly much quicker and the baby is at least sedated. So any son of mine is going to be circumcised by a mohel, preferably one medically qualified. But one last thought; I think it's absolutely appalling that medical science has failed to come up with a safe anaesthetic for newborn circumcisions."*

Chapter 3

David

During her second year in the nursing school, Kate made the acquaintance of a second year economics student at the university. David was in many ways very like Kate, bright, academically inclined and quite serious – but in career aspirations he was the more ambitious of the two. He planned to become a chartered accountant. He was not a number cruncher at heart, but believed that a C.A. qualification could be the launching pad for an interesting and well paid business career. Unlike Kate he was an only child. Kate and David came from similar family backgrounds socially and economically, both had professional parents, and they had attended comparable schools and held broadly similar political views. Neither family were churchgoers nor did they take much, if any, interest in religion, and David and Kate would probably have described themselves as agnostic had anyone been interested enough to enquire. In short, David and Kate came from compatible backgrounds, their families were compatible and they themselves found from the start that they were compatible. Although Kate and David hadn't met previously, their parents knew each other slightly and when they finally found out that their children had become friends, they were pleased on the principle that if their child had to get together with someone of the opposite sex – and they accepted somewhat grudgingly that it was bound to happen sooner or later, but preferably later – it might as well be with the offspring of a family they knew and approved of. They recognized that David and Kate were at an age when such friendships had to be expected. Accordingly the friendship was not discouraged by either set of parents but mildly encouraged from the start. Each set of parents liked their child's friend from their first meeting him or her, and was pleased their child's friend was easy to get along with and had excellent manners. In particular, David's mother took an immediate liking to Kate – she had always hoped that her son would find a really nice, well educated, intelligent and well brought up wife from a professional background and she saw Kate as fitting the bill perfectly. Kate's parents, for their part, considered David a very nice, kindly, intelligent young man from a good family whom they thought could be trusted to treat Kate well and, having had extensive experience of service life, were impressed that David had been commissioned during his national service which he had completed after leaving school and before going to university. Kate's father was grinning as he told her he wouldn't hold it against David that he'd chosen the Royal Air Force rather than the Royal Navy. "Thank you, Dad. Very big of you," said Kate, "and don't forget that when Churchill was talking about rum, sodomy and the lash he wasn't referring to the air force."

Over the next months the friendship between Kate and David progressed through romance to love and they came to regard themselves as informally engaged. This was in the days before the Pill and the relaxation of sexual conduct which its availability encouraged, indeed made possible. Their lovemaking progressed slowly and gradually from brief kisses on meeting and parting, then to longer, deeper ones while they were together and unobserved, then to Kate allowing David to touch her breasts briefly through her clothing, later to her permitting him to fondle her breasts (still clothed), thereafter to letting him caress her legs, first as far as her knees and subsequently the lower part of her thighs. Both of them had received liberal upbringings by contemporary standards, but Kate knew that her parents would certainly not allow her to take David into her bedroom, so she never tried. There were problems of privacy too; both lived at home under the eyes of their parents and Kate's home in particular offered the lovers little chance of seclusion when her brothers were home from their boarding schools – she was particularly wary of their nosiness.

So it was with difficulty that the physical side of their love made headway. Their love for one another had reached the point where they were talking of marriage when they had completed their studies and were self-supporting. Bike rides and walks in the surrounding countryside helped their lovemaking to become a little more adventurous. If they found a reasonably secluded spot Kate would allow David rather more freedom, but both were aware that everywhere they went was subject to access by other members of the public and neither relished the thought of their amorous activities being observed by anyone else – these precious, snatched moments had to be private. Even so, there were places and moments where, provided she could cover herself up quickly if the need arose, Kate would let David unbutton her blouse and undo her brassiere so that he could see, admire and caress her breasts and, as time went by, she also permitted him to kiss her breasts. Latterly she had permitted his hand to roam as far as the outside of the schoolgirl style panties she still wore, but to go inside her panties was verboten. She admitted to herself that she enjoyed everything that she allowed David to do to her at least as much as she thought David enjoyed it.

Chapter 4

Afternoon Tea

Kate realized that the relationship between her and David was and had to be a progressive one and, although she could within limits control the rate of progress, it could not be allowed to stand still for long periods. She was well aware, as he was, that they could not marry for several years to come since marriage was out of the question until they had qualified in their respective professions, got jobs and were economically self-sufficient. That meant she had to complete nursing school, pass her final exams and qualify for enrolment as a State Registered Nurse while David would have to get his degree, serve three years articles and pass his final exams to qualify as a chartered accountant. Then they would have to find jobs in the same area as each other. It was going to be a long haul. She felt sexually frustrated and she knew very well that David did, although he was too nice a person and too fond of her to force the pace or to try to persuade her to do anything that she felt was wrong or was uncomfortable with. She loved David and knew he loved her. She would not, could not, contemplate losing him. Love affairs had a momentum of their own, she reasoned, either they progressed to greater intimacy or the relationship would cool and, inevitably, end. She had to make a decision, and soon. She could perhaps slow the process by allowing David heavy petting sessions, provided they could find some place where privacy was assured, but heavy petting would, she thought, only increase their desire for each other. Realistically, she was sure progression would quickly lead to full intercourse. Was she ready for that? Kate had no moral qualms about losing her virginity before marriage. She thought that if a man really loved her - and she certainly wouldn't marry a man who didn't - he would marry her, virgin bride or not.

But her virginity was a gift she could confer only once. Was David the man she wanted to give it to? The only man she would ever want to give it to? Did she really love David? The answer to all three questions was "yes." She had answered her own dilemma.

But there was a problem which troubled her, one to which she knew most girls wouldn't give a second thought. Brought up with two circumcised brothers by a mother who had impressed on Kate from an early age very cogent views on the advisability of circumcision, views which had been reinforced by Kate's own reading, her observations and experiences as a nurse and exchanges of views with other nurses, including the common room and supper break discussions, Kate had concluded that circumcision in a man conferred hygienic and sexual benefits on him and his sexual partner and was aesthetically much more attractive. She had made up her mind that she would deliver the key to her door only to a circumcised lover.

But had David been circumcised? She had felt the bulge of his erection through his clothing when they were locked in embraces, but she hadn't seen him nude. She didn't know. She had wanted many times to ask him. She was in the position postulated by Jenny in the common room debate and, although Trish's riposte had been a bit coarse, she thought, it was a question which if asked might lead to unpredictable consequences. For this reason and because of her shyness she had so far restrained her curiosity, intense though it continued to be.

Kate had agreed with what had been said in the common room and at the supper break in favour of circumcision and in particular she had been struck by the forcefulness and candour of Margaret's comments in the common room. Margaret had expressed herself unequivocally as favouring the operation and said she was glad that her fiancé had been circumcised. If anyone could empathise with Kate's dilemma, Margaret would. She liked Margaret as a person. Margaret, a senior student, was someone she felt she could approach with confidence that she would get helpful advice, and not be laughed at. That evening she dropped by Margaret's room in the nurses' home. She tapped on the door rather nervously and Margaret's cheerful voice told her to come in.

Kate told her she needed some advice and hoped that Margaret would help her. "Of course," Margaret responded, "I hope I can help. Sometimes just talking a problem through with someone else means that you find your own answer. Do sit down. Now what's the matter, Kate?"

Kate told her of her love for David and that she had decided that their relationship had developed to the point that she wanted to go to bed with him, but there was this small snag; she felt like Margaret about the importance of circumcision and she didn't know whether he was circumcised. If he wasn't she would want him to have it done. Kate reminded Margaret of Jenny's intervention in the debate and, amid laughter on both sides at the recollection, Trish's prediction.

Margaret, able to be totally objective in a way that the lovelorn Kate was not, analysed Kate's problem, saying "Well, on a balance of probabilities, is David more likely to have been circumcised or not? Let's look at the facts. He was born in the early 1930s. Are his parents professional, working class or what? What kind of school did he go to – public school, council school or what?" Kate told Margaret that his parents were professionals, his mother a doctor, and that he had gone to prep and public schools. Margaret said she'd bet a week's pay that a doctor's son who had been educated at a public school would have been circumcised; either his attending a public school or his being a doctor's son on its own made it likely, she thought, but both combined made it very probable. "I don't think you've got anything to worry about, but if I'm wrong in my hunch and he isn't circumcised, don't issue an ultimatum – just say you hope he'll consider a circumcision. Let him mull it over and wait till he comes back to you on it. Remember, the fact you're asking such a question shows that you are sexually interested in him and could be seen as a big come-on, so, whatever you do, make sure you ask your question in a public place, but one where you have enough privacy and space that you won't be overheard. And, above all, DON'T ask him in mid-snog or without you both having ALL your clothes on – that way things could easily get out of control!"

Kate had shown Margaret her notes of the debate in the common room while reminding her of Jenny's questions and Trish's rejoinders. Later, as they had tea in her room, Margaret asked if she might read the notes through and, having read them, commented that she was glad the discussion had been recorded as she thought it had been a particularly good one, well argued, informative and enjoyable and, above all, on a topic which interested many nurses as it touched both their professional and private lives – not to mention its sexual implications. Margaret was editor of the nursing school gazette and told Kate she wished she could print Kate's account of the debate but even if it was edited to delete names she still couldn't publish it. What was left would reveal that the debaters were far more sexually active than the nursing school hierarchy probably believed, certainly more than it would wish to be known, and she feared a backlash and crackdown which would reduce their freedom. "Can you imagine what would happen if we published even a carefully edited and bowdlerised version of what was said in that debate? Not only did several participants deride and cast scorn on NHS policy against circumcision, which wouldn't please the school and hospital authorities who would, I'm afraid, be more likely to see and treat it as insubordination rather than a justifiable exercise in free speech, but Sister Starchy's worst fears would be confirmed and she'd be in the principal's office within minutes to tell her that the article proved Starchy's oft-expressed view that the sex life of the student body was worse than Sodom and Gomorrah combined, and that the principal owed it to the students' parents to protect their daughters from the sins of the flesh that this article proved beyond doubt they were indulging in on a grand scale. She'd demand formal vows of chastity from all students on admission and weekly virginity tests until graduation. Beyond graduation too, if she could swing it! It's a pity, Kate – that debate does deserve publication and would make far better reading than we usually achieve. I'm glad I've seen your note: it proves you are a good writer and reporter, so I would like you to join the Gazette staff and help with the Gazette." Kate told Margaret that she'd always wanted to write and would be delighted to come aboard – an invitation which in the event was to set Kate's feet firmly on the Gazette ladder, lead to wider recognition of her ability as a writer and boost her self-confidence. She became editor herself before she graduated from the nursing school.

Before Kate went to see Margaret she knew that her parents were planning a day trip away from home on either a Saturday or a Sunday in the near future; it was term time and both her brothers were away at boarding school. A house empty for a day offered possibilities, she thought.

Meanwhile she would find an opportunity to use Margaret's advice. She was cheered by Margaret's prediction that David would have been circumcised and the more she thought about it the more she felt that he would probably have been done as a baby. David's mother struck her as very much like her own and both her brothers had been done. But she couldn't be sure; she had to ask David.

Kate invited David to meet her for afternoon tea at a rather upmarket tea room they and other students couldn't afford to frequent, making her invitation sound rather casual – although she felt her heart beating far faster than usual – and saying it would be her treat. She had picked the tea room because her mother had taken her there and she remembered its spaciousness with the tables set well apart and the unobtrusive service. It promised privacy for the very personal question she wanted to put to David.

They met at the entrance to the tea room and Kate led the way to a table in an alcove well away from potential eavesdroppers. Kate, as we know, was a modest girl and although she was determined to put the question, even at this point, only minutes away from putting it, she still didn't know how to go about it. She had phrased and rephrased introductory words and The Question itself and held several private rehearsals, none of which had gone well. She had decided that she would rely upon the inspiration of the moment.

Once they had ordered and been served with tea and cakes, and using the interpersonal skills found more often and in greater measure in women than in men, she steered the conversation towards their relationship and reminded David that he was the only boyfriend that she had ever had. She told David that she had been nervous about telling her parents that she had met a boy she liked but the way they had taken to David had made things very easy, and his parents had been very nice to her, too. She and he had become very close; they contemplated marriage and she hoped it would come about. She told David that he had been very good in not trying to persuade her to go further than they had gone which she realized fell far short of what most unmarried couples they knew got up to. She realized that the restrictions they had observed must be as frustrating to him as they were to her and she hoped that he realized that she knew that they couldn't be as well behaved for evermore. She told him that she loved him and more than anything else in her life she wanted their relationship to continue and blossom into a happy marriage.

David responded by saying that he loved her very dearly and wanted to marry her as soon as they could support themselves. Within himself he was puzzled why she had invited him to this place she could ill afford. He was sure Kate's remarks were a prelude to something important. Something must be worrying her. What was she leading up to? But what could it be?

Now or never, thought Kate a bit desperately, but how on earth do I ask him? If only I didn't feel so strongly about it – I'm sure most girls, even nurses, don't.

Gathering her courage together and hoping that she could get it out without breaking down in embarrassment in mid-speech, she began, "David, darling, there's something which I feel very strongly about, although it may seem very trivial to you, and which I would like to ask you. It's a very, very, personal question." David broke in and said, "Look, we're talking about marriage and spending the rest of our lives together. There's nothing which you should feel you can't ask me. If there's anything, anything at all, which you want to know, please ask without bottling it up and agonizing about it for a moment longer." He wanted to take her in his arms and reassure her about whatever was troubling her, but he couldn't do that here. He would have to wait until she could bring herself to ask whatever it was that she was struggling to ask. Whatever it was.

Kate paused to ratchet her courage up one final notch and said, "Look, David, you're going to laugh at me when I ask you, but do please remember that I'm a nurse and nurses have their own pet worries which are not always the same as other people's." David felt more puzzled than ever about what was concerning her. She hesitated for several seconds, looked anxiously at him, looked around to make sure she wouldn't be overheard, looked at him again, this even more anxiously, then bravely plunged on. "David, darling, what I want to know is whether you have been circumcised."

She was still looking anxiously at David. His face was a picture. He had had no idea what Kate's remarks were leading up to except that it was something that was troubling her, and probably had been worrying her for some time, and this was all it was. His first instinct was to laugh, out of sheer relief that it was nothing serious that was causing her concern, but that wouldn't do – it would hurt her feelings if he laughed about something that was troubling her. Here was this demure girl asking a very undemure question. Then it struck him what an effort it would have been for someone so modest and shy to ask it. Plainly it was a matter of serious importance to her – he could tell that from her expression. He loved her. He must not laugh. He must keep his face very straight indeed. He must answer her question. He must tell her the truth, whether it was what she wanted to hear or what she didn't want to hear. But what answer was she hoping to hear? No matter, he must tell her for better or for worse.

"Yes," he replied. "Yes. I have been. When I was a baby."

He was glad to see the concerned look vanish immediately from her face to be instantly replaced by an expression of evident relief.

"Thank you," she said. "I'm so happy."

"Kate, darling, is that all that was worrying you? Is there anything else you want to know?"

"No. Honestly. That's all. You've told me what I hoped to hear."

David was very intrigued but decided not to pursue the matter there and then. There would be other places and times more appropriate than a tea room for exploring Kate's sexual preferences which might lead to activities both would enjoy. Meanwhile he must content himself with the realisation that the very nature and intimacy of Kate's question and her obvious approval of his answer coupled with what she had said before asking the question meant that their relationship was moving into a new, overtly sexual phase. He felt enormously happy.

Chapter 5

Reflection

Kate felt exhilarated as she went home from the tea room. She now knew that she wanted to surrender her virginity to David. As soon as possible. When she did so she now knew that he would be the lover of her dreams in every respect.

Her brothers being away at boarding school, she had sole tenure of the bathroom she shared with them and that night she could enjoy the luxury of a really leisurely soak in the bath while she mused on a momentous day.

After undressing in her bedroom, she pulled on her dressing gown and entered the bathroom. She filled the bath and added some of the bath salts she had received as a gift last Christmas and had been saving for a special occasion. Standing in front of the long mirror, she untied the belt of her dressing gown and let the garment slide slowly from her shoulders to the floor. What she could see reflected in the mirror was what David would see when he first saw her in the nude. She hoped he wouldn't feel disappointed. She had never thought of herself as a beauty – her brothers had seen to that – but looking at herself critically she thought that the body she hoped to offer to David in the near future wasn't too bad. He shouldn't feel about her as Henry VIII had felt about Anne of Cleeves or George IV about Caroline of Brunswick, she thought. True, she hadn't got the kind of bountiful bosom that some girls had, but once when she had allowed David to caress her breasts and she had commented self-deprecatingly on their size in comparison with a mutual acquaintance's, hadn't he whispered that quality was more important than quantity? She studied the image of her body in the mirror, turning through 90 degrees sideways as she did so. Her breasts were small, she admitted to herself, but they were reasonably well formed, she hoped. She gave herself a 180 degree turn in the opposite direction, viewed her reflection, and then swivelled back towards the mirror. She hoped that he wouldn't be disappointed by her breasts. Her hips were very slim, almost boyish, matching her upper works. She thought to herself that, although she was far from voluptuous and would probably disappoint some men by that fact, she wasn't badly proportioned and she hoped that David would continue to put quality ahead of quantity when he saw her au naturel.

She stepped into the bath and sat soaping her breasts, torso, arms and legs before lowering herself to lie full-length in the bath with her head resting against the end of the bath.

As she lay there, she tried to vizualise what making love with David was going to be like – she was sure now it was going to happen quite soon. She had allowed him to kiss her bare breasts. That had thrilled her and she had felt her nipples react by becoming erect, but she had never had the opportunity to allow him more than a brief encounter with her bare bosom and she did not know just how excited she might get in a prolonged rendezvous between her naked breasts and his mouth with its questing tongue. From his kissing her breasts, which she had at least experienced briefly, her mind wandered to a form of kissing she hadn't yet experienced, but knew from common room chatter to be popular among couples. What would it feel like if – no, she thought, when – she allowed him to kiss her between her legs, that most secret area, a freedom she knew many girls only permitted to their husbands or boyfriends as the greatest intimacy of all, the final revelation of the mysteries of the female body, and usually, she believed, a privilege accorded only after they had surrendered their virginities? The thought excited her and became more exciting as she wondered again what David would think when he first saw her completely nude. She kept her pubic area, as well as her legs, arms and underarms, completely free of hair by regular shaving and the use of depilatory creams, and now she asked herself whether David would prove to be one of those males who were said to be turned on by the presence of pubic hair, rather than its absence. She suffered a twinge of doubt. In its natural state the genital area was concealed by a mat of pubic hair. She herself had always thought body hair on women unsightly but now she allowed herself to wonder whether men found it sexy. After all, as she knew from her hospital experience, most married women didn't go to the trouble of removing it – could it be that their husbands were turned on by the sight of pubic hair and actually preferred them hairy? When shaved she knew her most intimate parts would be on view to her lover and perhaps she would feel vulnerable in a way she would not feel if she allowed her pubic hair to grow. So what, she thought, if I'm going to give him access I'm going to want to make him feel welcome and won't he feel more welcome if he realizes that I have shaved myself to give him a clear view of my most secret parts and easier access to them with his penis and his mouth and tongue? Anyway, hair must get in the way, she thought - can any man pleasuring a woman orally really want to get a mouthful of hair and find his lips and tongue scratched by hair? She wanted to render his making love to her as easy and enjoyable as possible. As to vulnerability, she loved David and she wanted to surrender herself sexually to him, so she would positively wish to feel vulnerable to him when they were about to make love, particularly for the first time. When allowed, he had caressed her bare legs and each time, she remembered, he had commented in a whisper on the smoothness of her skin. She was quite sure this meant he would prefer a hairless body, and she made a mental note to do a really thorough removal of all traces of body hair immediately before any occasion when circumstances might make nudity possible.

Then, having finally resolved any lingering doubts she might have had about her desire to present David with a totally hairless body, she tried to visualize David kissing her most intimate parts – and they would be free from any hair - hoping that he would begin on her tummy and move his mouth slowly downwards to the front of one of her thighs, then to an inner thigh and slowly up to the cleft of her vulva. There she hoped he would kiss the lips of her labia and that they would both feel the lips of her labia part of their own accord to open the long slit of her vulva to his exploring tongue. What, she wondered, would his tongue protruding into her vulva feel like as it moved towards the exquisitely sensitive region of her clitoris, lingering there, she hoped, and then moving as it sought to find the entrance to her vagina? Only at that moment, as she lay there in the bath did it strike her that by grasping his head with her hands she would be able to steer his mouth and tongue to the parts of her that most urgently demanded his attention. That was a happy and reassuring thought. The water was warm and soon after, lulled her from her reverie into a light sleep.

Awakening, she lay in the bath allowing herself now the luxury of imagining having all her clothing removed item by item by David. She hoped that he would bare her breasts before he removed her panties – she thought it would be more seemly if her pubic area, her most intimate zone, remained clothed until the last. After all, her virginity was the greatest gift she could give David. Having settled to her satisfaction the sequence in which she looked forward to being divested of every stitch of her own apparel and resolving that on any occasion when divestment seemed possible, it would be as well to be wearing garments as few in number and as easily removed as possible, she turned her mind to how she would undress David as he disrobed her. It would be a sequence in which the final divestment would be his underpants. But her mind couldn't concentrate as it should on planning the undressing because she had no idea what he would be wearing. All she really needed to remember was that his underpants, like her panties, should be the last item and that they should come off at the same time as or very soon after she had yielded her panties. The warmth of the water was making her sleepy again and she was trying to visualize what David would look like in the nude. He was slimly built, just as she was herself. She was fortunate as a nurse to have a much better idea than most other virgins of what her lover's sexual parts would look like. Thanks to that memorable visit to the tea room today she could put one more piece in the jigsaw, but when she first saw him, would he be erect or flaccid?

She was getting really sleepy now, her mind woozy and apt to wander, but she made the effort to summon up one more thought; she hoped that his undressing her as she undressed him would result in his being so sexually aroused that the first moment she saw him entirely nude his penis – and she now knew that it would be a circumcised penis – would be fully erect. Rampant, she said to herself, sleepily but very happily. She smiled at the thought.

The water was now cooler and she made the effort to rouse herself so that she could top up the bath with the hot tap. That done, she lay back in the bath to resume her reverie. With it came the realization that she and David might be "going all the way," as she put it to herself, very, very soon now. She was a virgin, as was David. She was a nurse and more knowledgeable than most virgins and it was up to her to make sure that their first intercourse was as enjoyable for both of them as possible and as nearly as possible pain free for her. She wanted him to penetrate her as easily as possible – that way he would be less likely to reach a climax and ejaculate before he had entered her fully – and this first time she wanted very much to feel him reach orgasm with his penis fully inside her vagina and preferably not too quickly, so that she too attained a climax. She was glad that she had taken her mother's advice to use tampons rather than sanitary towels. Penetration shouldn't be a big problem, she hoped. She picked up the tube of surgical jelly she had brought from its hiding place in her underwear drawer and, having unscrewed the cap, she put a liberal dollop on the end of her forefinger and inserted her finger gently in the opening of her vagina. For a long while she lay in the bath gently stretching the entrance partly closed by her hymen and continued until she was satisfied that she had widened it significantly. She resolved to make a practice of having a late night bath and continuing this treatment, which she admitted to herself was very pleasant, until she and David had made love.

By now very sleepy again, her hand slipped on to her clitoris and she began to caress herself very gently as she lay in the bath thinking about David.

En Passant

There was a rather battered old armless wooden chair with a narrow seat in the kitchen of Kate's parents' house. It had been there as far back as Kate could remember and was already an old chair when her parents acquired it before she was born. It was one of those articles that people find useful and, however old-fashioned and battered they become, never replace because they can't be improved upon for the humble but useful services to which they are put. So the old chair had become a permanent part of the scene in which Kate grew up and it went on to play its part in several episodes in Kate's life. So much so that after the chair became Kate's she could never be persuaded to part with it. Only she and David knew why.

Chapter 6

Revelation

It was term time and both Kate's brothers were away at boarding school, so when her parents told her that they were going on their day long outing the next day and would be making an early start, Kate wasted no time in phoning David to invite him to spend the following day with her, but did not mention that they would have the house to themselves. They arranged that David would arrive at 10 am.

Kate had a surprise in mind for David. She had preparations to make. That night before she went to bed she carefully shaved off any traces of body hair to a pre-op standard that nursing experience had taught her the most exacting theatre sister would applaud. After her parents left the next morning after an early breakfast, she shaved herself again "just to make sure," bathed, took the old armless wooden chair which had rather a narrow seat from the kitchen to her bedroom, "borrowed" from the airing cupboard an oldish towel which she thought her mother wouldn't miss and settled down to apply her make-up with particular care. Then she put on a favourite sundress with a halter top which David had admired and had the advantage of making a bra superfluous. She put on a pair of very brief panties she had bought the day before but, after a moment's reflection, she took them off and put them back in her underwear drawer. It was nearly 10, and she was ready for what she knew would be an unforgettable day.

When David rang the doorbell, Kate opened the door to him and they got no further than the entrance hall before they stopped for a kiss which led to another and another. As they kissed, David's hand had crept via her breast down to the hem of her skirt and from there up her leg. At the point that David had come to expect to find her panties he found to his surprise and delight only skin, but Kate gently lifted his hand away and said in a husky voice so low as to be almost a whisper "David, darling, I've got a confession to make and I hope you won't mind, but with Mum and Dad away for the day we've got the house to ourselves until seven tonight. I've run a bath upstairs. Would you like to share it with me?"

David was almost lost for words. "Oh yes! Oh yes! What an absolutely super idea!" and he kissed the beautiful girl he loved who was offering him this blissful encounter before they rushed upstairs to her bedroom, he thankful that without any serious expectation of the good fortune which now awaited him he had taken the precaution of buying a packet of Durex. What he didn't know was that after the tea room meeting Kate had, with the connivance of a more worldly colleague, obtained a similar packet as well as the tube of surgical jelly.

In the bedroom they were held up by the need to kiss, felt more urgently by both than ever before. The halter of Kate's sundress was soon undone and revealed her small, beautifully formed breasts with their cute little nipples to his admiring gaze. She pulled his shirt over his head. He bent and kissed each of her breasts in turn in a series of spirals of decreasing radius before arriving at the nipple which he gently took into his mouth, where to his great joy he felt it stiffen.

Kate unbuckled his belt and unzipped his pants and found and caressed the bulge in David's underpants. Her caress was gentle and brief because she feared anything more might cause David to go off prematurely and she didn't want any accident of that sort. She wondered how to manoeuvre the elasticated waistband of his underpants over his erect, engorged organ. Simultaneously, David was worrying about the mechanics of removing Kate's sundress but happily he found the zip fastener at the back just as Kate concluded that by pulling the waistband of his underpants towards her and then downwards she could complete his undressing without any risk of hurting him.

So it was that each achieved the other's complete nudity at the same time. They kicked away the garments encircling their ankles, followed by their sandals. They stood kissing each other before, rather shyly, each looked downwards – David to take in the beauty of Kate's breasts with their erect nipples and her lovely hairless mons and Kate to see a penis brought, as she realized with delight, to a high state of excitement by her very proximity to him and the depth of his love and desire for her. Kate was conscious of moisture between her legs. She was ready for him. And she could see he was ready for her.

Then Kate, feeling very excited indeed, led an equally excited David by the hand into the bathroom – she had felt a momentary temptation to lead him by his penis but the last vestiges of maidenly modesty prevailed. Still holding his hand she climbed into the bath, and David knelt on the floor by it as she seated herself in the warm water. He gently washed her breasts with a well soaped hand, exclaiming with pleasure at their beauty before, with his arm supporting her shoulders, he lowered her into a recumbent position and began to bathe her flat tummy and slender thighs. As he washed caressingly an inner thigh she felt her excitement mounting and eased her thighs apart so that he could soap the area between her legs. And so at last he came to her beautiful mons and vulva. He lathered them gently and lingeringly. Then she put her hand over his and guided his movements showing him first her clitoris and then the hymen which, she explained huskily and very quietly, still partly covered the entrance to her vagina, all the while feeling her own excitement mount still further. And she sensed the pleasure David was not only giving her but receiving himself from what he was doing to her.

Then, still quietly but with excitement obvious in the huskiness of her whisper, she asked David to get in the bath with her so that she could wash and explore him as he had so lovingly washed and explored her. She sat up in the bath as he knelt facing her with his erection jutting upwards and towards her. Although she had felt his erection pressing against her through his clothes several times while kissing, this was the first time she had seen an erect adult penis and she experienced a moment of panic at the size of his engorged organ and the thought of accommodating it within her, wondering whether the loss of her virginity was going to be painful. But recollections of conversations with her more experienced friends and anatomy lectures at the nursing school speedily came to her aid and she also remembered that she had stretched her hymen in preparation for this very event. All will be well, she said to herself. What a nicely shaped penis he has, she thought, and no surplus skin at all.

Kate reached for David's penis and took it gently, very gently, into her hand. His penis was erect and hard to her touch, engorged with blood, yet the greyish-pink head had a velvety feel to it. Just below the flaring, mushroom shaped head she found the line which she was looking for, a very faint whitish-grey line running right round his penis. She told David in a whisper how very happy she was that he had been circumcised. Speaking very quietly and huskily, she said he had a lovely looking penis with a nicely shaped head and had had just the right amount of skin cut away to leave him with a neat, very regular but almost invisible scar line and no excess skin at all. "Just what this nurse would have asked for," she added. Did David's penis swell even further in appreciation of her remarks or was it her imagination? Strange, isn't it, she thought, that a girl as shy and reserved as I am – or was – wants to say things like this to a man who only minutes ago I hadn't seen nude and hadn't seen me nude. Still clasping his penis gently and still almost in a whisper, she told David that both her brothers had been circumcised and her mother had impressed on her that circumcision was an aid to hygiene. When they made love his circumcision would delay his climax and this would help her to attain her orgasm. In her opinion, circumcision made a penis look much nicer and its greater cleanliness would be beneficial to her own health as well as his. "I think it looks lovely," she concluded still whispering huskily.

By now Kate was washing his penis and scrotum with a

well soaped hand and very gently indeed to ensure that she did not bring him to a climax there and then, as Kate intended that his climax should not occur until David's penis was fully inside her vagina, and preferably as she reached her own orgasm.

Both Kate and David were now wondering about how to tackle the other about what each knew to be the next item on the agenda. There was magic in the air and neither wanted to risk spoiling this most precious moment in their lives. David was agonizing whether to tell her about the condoms he had brought and, if so, what to say, but it was Kate who put him out of the state of misery which, very comparatively speaking, had suddenly beset him, ecstatic with his good fortune that he otherwise was.

"Darling, you know I love you and hope one day we will marry, but we can't think of marrying until we've both finished our training and got jobs. We've gone this far and if we don't make love now, we are both going to be horribly frustrated – I know I would be. We are lucky, very lucky, that we don't have to worry about taking precautions, thank goodness, as today is a safe day in my cycle and I'm as regular as clockwork. You will have to be a bit patient this first time in easing your way past my hymen, but I've got some surgical jelly for lubrication, and I do want you to make love to me today. I've been looking forward to it ever since Mum said they'd be away all day today and I phoned you."

David was, of course, delighted that the girl he loved should actually be inviting him to do to her what he so ardently wanted to do. He was being spared something he had secretly agonized about recently; he had long wanted to make love to her, but he had been uneasy about taking the lead, involving, as he expected it would, the need for him to take the initiative in persuading her to do something which, even if she acquiesced, she might well have had qualms about. He expressed his enormous delight to her and then, rather shamefacedly, confessed that he had brought a packet of condoms with him but only as a precaution with no expectation that he would be allowed to use them, and he admitted that the need for surgical jelly had not occurred to him.

Very erect now, David climbed out of the bath and gave his hand to assist Kate to follow him. Delightful as their occupation of the bath had been, even greater pleasure was now at the forefront of their minds. They dried each other with towels, hastily and a little perfunctorily, and Kate remembered to dab herself with talc. Then, throwing her previous modesty and all shyness to the winds, Kate grasped her lover's erect organ gently in her hand and led the way into her bedroom.

Student Nurse Kate had thought carefully about the mechanics of losing her virginity with an emphasis on the maximum of pleasure and the minimum of discomfort. She had finally decided against losing it while lying on her back in bed, although that seemed to be the usual way. She wanted to be able to control the rate of entry of her lover's penis and it was with this in mind that she had "borrowed" the old, wooden chair with its narrow seat and no arms – which seemed ideal, she thought, for the purpose - from her mother's kitchen and put it in her bedroom where it now stood prominently, and somewhat incongruously, in the middle of the floor. She produced the tube of surgical jelly from its hiding place at the bottom of her underwear drawer, put the tube in the washbasin and filled the basin with hot water so that the jelly would be warm when needed. They stood momentarily and kissed. Then she pulled away from him and sat on the edge of the bed telling David in her low husky voice what she thought would be the easiest way for him to make love to her virginal self. After this she lowered her head and torso backwards on to the bed and slowly opened her legs. Without waiting for any further invitation and knowing instinctively what she wanted him to do, David knelt on the floor between her legs and as he lowered his head to kiss her she extended her arms towards him and grasped his head between her hands. She guided him first to the lower part of her tummy and then one of her thighs, allowing him to move to the inside of the thigh before letting him work his way upwards to her lovely immaculately shaven mons and then insert his tongue into the cleft of her vulva and very gently kiss her with his tongue between her labial lips moving from the area of her clitoris towards the entrance to her vagina. Kate was moaning gently, and David realized happily that she was signalling pleasure. David could feel how wet she was becoming and, aware that she was fast approaching her orgasm, Kate released David's head and whispered to him to pass her the tube of jelly lying in the washbasin. She unscrewed the cap and, using her index finger, deposited the warm jelly in the entrance of her vagina.

Kate sat up and then they stood, embracing and kissing each other with a passion engendered by what had passed between them already that morning and sharpened immeasurably by their thoughts on what they were about to do when they consummated their love. Kate could feel David's erection pressing against her tummy as they stood locked together. Then, speaking as calmly as she could but if anything more huskily than before, she asked David to sit on the old chair, picked up the jelly tube and knelt in front of him.

As she knelt there she realized that this was a minute in her life which could never be repeated; she was about to lose for ever her virginity and she wanted to savour the event, to record it in her mind for all time as a mental snapshot. There, in front of her, waiting for her was David, his lovely penis as erect as a flagstaff, as rigid as it ever could be with the glans as bare and the skin on the shaft stretched as taut as any combination of circumcision and erection could make them. "Just as it should be," she thought to herself happily as she concentrated on the scene determined to remember it, "my circumcised lover ready and eager to take the virginity I am giving him." She gently grasped his penis and pulled downwards on the skin covering the shaft as with her other hand she coated the head with jelly from the tube. Then, dropping the tube on the floor and still holding his very erect penis in her hand, she stood and moved forward to straddle his thighs, then bent her knees to lower herself towards the waiting penis, simultaneously using her hand to guide it into the entrance to her vagina. "Courage!" she whispered to herself, as his penis met the resistance of her hymen, but the pleasure and excitement she was experiencing far outweighed any discomfort she felt as she continued to lower herself against the slight resistance and very soon she announced triumphantly to David, "Darling, you're fully inside me. And it feels lovely."

Miraculously - and afterwards he was proud of this achievement in self-control because he too was very excited - he had managed so far to defer his orgasm. He asked Kate if she would like to move to her bed. Kate herself, silently congratulating him on not having already ejaculated despite his obvious excitement at penetrating her, was thinking that making love in bed would be much more comfortable and rewarding than on the chair, admirably though it had served a purpose for which it had not been designed. Kate agreed, gently disengaged herself and stood, followed by David. They walked hand in hand to her bed – "our nuptial couch" as she thought to herself happily. As Kate pulled the top sheet and blankets down, moved the pillow half way down the bed to support her hips and laid the purloined bath towel to protect the pillow, David anxiously asked whether his entering her had hurt her or made her sore; to his great relief she said it hadn't and added that it had been a wonderful, unforgettable experience and she wanted to resume where they had left off. Then she hugged him to her before she got on the bed, and there, lying on her back with her hips raised by the pillow and her legs parted, with David above her and lying between her thighs, she again guided David's penis into its new home. She brought her legs over his thighs so that their bodies were locked together as tightly as their desire for each other could contrive. The two of them lay there joined in a loving embrace, moving gently in unison and savouring each other and the new feelings they were experiencing together. They both came explosively, and almost simultaneously.

Afterwards, they lay there side by side, exchanging many prolonged kisses, his hands cupping her breasts and she with one hand clasping and encircling his penis below the head, causing it after a while to become erect again. Later they got up and, without dressing, had a snack in the kitchen. Before they returned to the bedroom David asked Kate again if she was in any discomfort and after she said she was alright they went back to bed where they made love again after Kate had re-anointed her lover's penis with jelly to ease its passage on this third entry into her. They both achieved climaxes - Kate's being quite a noisy one.

After that they relaxed in bed in each other's arms and, as they lay satiated and happy, Kate took David's temporarily limp penis in her hand and gently ran the nail of her forefinger round the shaft just below the glans. His penis stirred at her touch and, emboldened, she reminded him that it was only a few days ago that she had learned that he was circumcised. "I know it seems silly now, but I was far too shy to ask previously whether you had been done. When we were in the bath I told you how glad I was that you had had a circumcision. Truth to tell, I was very, very relieved when you answered my question in the tea room. If you hadn't been circumcised I would have wanted you to have it done before we started to live together and I didn't know how you would feel about that nor how I would have gone about asking you. You don't know the relief I felt when you told me that you had been circumcised as a baby."

Kate had grown up very fast that day and now she did something she would not have thought possible twenty four hours before. While she was talking David's penis had become very erect again and she leant over him, her cute little breasts hanging vertically, kissed his glans and took it into her mouth. Then, being a nurse as well as a romantic at heart, a passing thought struck her and she disengaged her lips from his penis just long enough to enquire in her husky whisper "Darling, would you have any objection to any son of ours being circumcised? Just like you?" David tried to collect his thoughts as well as he in the delightful situation of having his penis in this lovely and loving girl's mouth could do. "Well," he murmured, "it's the woman who's the consumer. You are a consumer right now, aren't you? What do you think?" Kate lifted her head rather reluctantly to reply. "I love your circumcision and after today I would not be happy if any son of ours had his little helmet covered for any longer than it takes to arrange to uncover it permanently." Her mouth went back to his penis and she lapped it again with her tongue but suddenly stopped and whispered, "No. No. Not right away. I would want his circumcision to wait until after I'd passed my six week post-partum check up and been cleared to make love again. That way we could celebrate in an appropriate way the fact that I was a woman with not just one but two naked helmets in my life."

Prudently, but with extreme reluctance, they got up well ahead of Kate's parents' expected time of arrival, returned the kitchen chair – always to be an object of affection to them in the future – to its accustomed place in the kitchen, removed any trace of their occupation of the bath, returned an unblemished, refolded towel to its storage place, remade Kate's bed with immaculate hospital corners fashioned by Kate and re-hid the tube of jelly with the unused condoms in her underwear drawer. David told Kate that for him the day had been the most wonderful day of his life and an experience which had made him love her even more than before and she responded by saying that she felt the same way. David forced himself to leave before Kate's parents returned, leaving a happy Kate to relive in her mind over and over again the events of the day in which she passed from girlhood into womanhood and to reflect on the love which David and she felt for each other and had consummated that day.

Chapter 7

Sequel

Kate's parents didn't leave their house free for use by Kate and David by going away very often, but whenever it happened and her brothers were away at school the lovers took full advantage of their brief freedom and became quite adept at altering their hospital and university schedules at short notice. They never got caught.

Another opportunity came only a week after their first day together. Kate's parents decided to spend another day away from home and the lovers' day followed very much the pattern of that wonderful first day, beginning with a leisurely bath together and the rest of the day in bed, broken only by a snack to recharge their batteries and keep up their energy levels. Following the same pattern didn't mean they lacked imagination but rather that they had enjoyed themselves so much the first time and because for them there was no better way to spend their limited time together.

This second time was much freer from tension, freed as they were from any nervousness natural to making love for the first time, and each felt more relaxed in relating to the other, but this time Kate was at a point in her cycle when there was a risk of conception and she warned him they had to use a condom. Neither was too worried by the possibility of having an orgasm sooner than they would have wished because they now knew that one orgasm could be followed by another, although in David's case he needed time to recover before he could attain another erection. So they were more active in stimulating each other and, practice making perfect, even better lovemaking resulted on this second day together.

In her bedroom, they first took their shoes off and then undressed each other, hugging, kissing and caressing as their clothes came off to reveal the bodies they had explored with so much pleasure a week previously. This time, Kate was wearing a jumper and shorts and David lifted the jumper over her head to find a bra that needed to be unhooked before he could caress her breasts and feel her nipples stiffen as he kissed them. He unzipped her shorts and pulled them down as she undid his belt and zipper and relieved him of his trousers. Her panties followed her shorts and she pulled his underpants down to reveal the throbbing erection she knew would await her. Unceremoniously and impatiently they kicked away the clothing encumbering their ankles. David knelt to kiss her mons and, rising, led her towards the bed where they lay for a while kissing and cuddling before they started to pay attention to those specific parts of the body which demanded to be caressed and kissed. Kate's breasts were lovingly fondled and her nipples sucked into erection and David's hand crept softly over her tummy and down the inside of a thigh before its journey ended at the hairless cleft he had come to adore, while her hand sought his penis and she encircled it with her hand which she moved gently down the engorged head and shaft, as she marvelled again at the firmness of his erection. As they lay there, David said how grateful he was that she had invited him to her house last week and now again and remarked on how much more they each now knew about the other, mentally as well as physically, than previously. Then he said, "I always knew you'd look beautiful without your clothes on, but I didn't realize just how incredibly beautiful. You're so well proportioned. You look absolutely wonderful." He kissed her breasts as she continued to hold his penis, caressing it gently. Then he said, "Let's have another wonderful bath together, like last week. It's so intimate."

Kate climbed into the bath first and as David followed her she said, "I love the look of your penis. It's so unwrinkled and neat and I'm glad it's a normal size – I wouldn't want one any larger than yours, it's a perfect fit for me." While they were in the bath they knelt facing each other as each washed the other, less shy this time than during their first bath together. Kate had shaved before David's arrival and as she was washing David's penis, a happy thought struck her and she said, "We must be the nudest couple in the world at this moment. My body is newly shaved and you were so beautifully circumcised that whether you are erect as you now are or fully relaxed your glans is always completely bare and there's no excess skin on your shaft." David carried her thought forward, "Well, isn't it right that two people in love like us shouldn't hide anything from each other? Neither of us is hiding anything, and I like that, don't you?"

Their second bath together was both more carefree and less carefree than the first. This time, Kate did not have to worry about the possibility of pain on David entering her and both had a confidence about satisfying the other which was lacking while they were in the bath the previous week, but on this occasion they had to learn how to use a condom. It made them appreciate how fortunate they had been that their first intercourse had occurred, by luck rather than by design, during one of Kate's safe periods. David helped Kate out of the bath and they hugged each other and kissed while they dried each other, and he told her again that she was quite incredibly beautiful when nude. He was still concerned that she might be sore from her first sexual encounter a week before but she assured him she was fine. Then they went into Kate's room and David unwrapped a Durex which he rather shyly asked Kate to put on his penis. He was worried that he might go into orgasm as the wretched thing went on but was encouraged by the fact that he had managed to deflower Kate, penetrate her for a second time and last for a measurable time within her vagina before he had climaxed a week ago. Kate deftly unrolled the condom on to his erect penis without incident, to their joint relief, and explained that she had attended classes where the nursing students had been taught the rudiments of family planning including the technique of putting a condom on. "I didn't know then how soon I would be putting my new skill to use," she said with a big grin. Then, shyly and a little hesitantly, she spoke again, "Would you mind very much kissing my vulva using your mouth and tongue before you come into me? It was so wonderfully exciting when you did it to me last week." David drew her to him and kissed her before saying he would love to do so. She pulled the bedding down and lay across the bed on her back and, as he knelt by the side of the bed facing her, she parted her legs, exposing her vulva to his questing tongue, but this time she placed her legs on his shoulders. She moaned immediately he kissed her vulva and continued to do so as she clasped his head with her thighs and her hands and pulled it closer to the cleft his tongue was exploring and which was getting ever wetter with their mingled secretions. Her hips began to gyrate and, realising that she was close to climax, she gasped, "Darling David, please give me the jelly now!" He quickly grabbed the tube of jelly from the washbasin where she had put it to warm and handed it to her. She hastily applied a generous quantity to the entrance of her vagina. Then he moved her so that he could get on to the bed and kneel between her knees as she lay waiting for him on her back with her hips raised by the pillow she was lying on. She took the jelly tube again and applied a coating to his Durex-covered penis before guiding his penis into her vagina which clasped it like a well-fitting glove. With her legs over his thighs they moved in unison, he gently as he was still unsure about hurting her if he moved vigorously, and he asked her, "Darling, I'm not hurting you, am I?" and she replied, "No, darling, I can take more thrusting if you'd like to do me like that. I'll tell you if it's too much." He began to experiment with longer and shorter and faster and slower movements of his penis and monitored her responses as well as he could until eventually she said, "That's lovely – I think that's how I'll always want to be done. Thank you, darling, for being such a thoughtful lover. You make me so happy. And, as I said in the bath, your penis is just the right size for me."

Later, still in bed, Kate spent time explaining the role of her clitoris in bringing her to orgasm and the extreme sensitivity of the clitoris which meant that too much direct stimulation caused discomfort rather than pleasure, but when he asked if he had been too rough, she assured him that she had felt only pleasure on both occasions when he had gone down on her. She showed David how best to stimulate the clitoral area. She lay back and helped David to explore gently her vagina with his finger coated with the surgical jelly. David was still concerned that he might have hurt her when entering her and asked her, but she assured him that it hadn't hurt. She had thought it might be painful the first time they made love, but her stretching her hymen beforehand must have made the passage of his penis easier and she felt no more pain than if, say, he had rapped her with no great force on her arm. She rapped his arm to illustrate what she meant. "It was a really lovely experience – no pain, just the sensation of your glans pressing against the entrance to my vagina, then its entry into my vagina and, finally, my vagina full of your rigid penis. I felt no pain, just the faintest discomfort as the head of your penis stretched my hymen and that was quickly over, as I said. The feeling that I shall always remember was one of joy that you were making love to me. Nor was I sore afterwards when you re-entered me and later when we made love again. It's all just a lovely memory with no negative factors at all. Today, when you entered me there was no discomfort at all – just a lovely, joyous feeling."

As they lay there, Kate asked him about the things he liked best and how she could play with his penis and give him the maximum pleasure without hurting him – she said she appreciated that there was a thin line between pleasure and pain. By experimenting at his very prompt invitation, she found out how much pressure should be used to pull the skin down the shaft of his penis and practised the delicate art of arriving at a balance between too much downward pressure (which would cause him pain) and just enough (which gave him exquisite pleasure). She learned from him with some surprise that his glans was actually less sensitive than the sulcus, the skin covering the groove immediately below his glans, but then she realized that the glans deprived by his circumcision of the protection afforded by a foreskin had become toughened and made less sensitive by the action of clothing brushing against it. His glans had changed colour from its original pink as a baby to its present greyish hue because of this toughening process, which she knew was called keratinisation. Growing up freed from the restraint of a foreskin, his circumcision would have had the effect of giving him a larger glans resulting in her circumcised lover being able to give the wall of her vagina more stimulation. Also, she benefited from the fact that David's circumcision had removed sufficient skin to ensure that his glans was fully exposed at all times while in the vagina so that friction was not reduced by the corona, or rim, of the glans being covered at any point during the movement of his penis within her vagina. All these factors gave her promise of greater sexual satisfaction during lovemaking from a circumcised lover like David, than from one who had not had this trivial operation.

That day loosened more inhibitions. The week before, when Kate had wanted to pee she had gone into the bathroom on her own. Today when David needed a pee she went with him and grasped his penis to aim the flow into the lavatory bowl. Unfortunately David immediately became aroused and his erection shut off the stream so they had to wait until his erection subsided before Kate could help him perform. After he'd finished, Kate couldn't resist manipulating him as he stood there to find out how quickly she could give him another erection. Then, rather shyly, she whispered that she needed a leak too and grasped his hand so that he would know that she would like him to stay with her. To advance his education, she didn't sit down on the lavatory seat as she would ordinarily have done but instead stood astride it so that he could see her perform and the stream she produced. David appreciated, as he had so often during their two days together, the efforts that Kate, shy and modest by nature and upbringing, was making to get rid of any inhibitions she had which might constitute barriers to intimacy between them. He appreciated more than ever the kind and caring nature of the beautiful girl he loved and who so obviously loved him.

As they lay in bed after they had made love for the first, but not the last, time that day, they caressed each other, each gradually learning what gave the other the most pleasure and equally important – because they had agreed to be totally honest with each other – what to avoid, and how to improve the sensations felt by the other. It was this desire to learn how to please each other that prompted Kate to ask David if he would prefer her to keep her pubic area shaved or whether he would like her to let the hair grow back. He said he loved her just as she was; the naked cleft of her vulva looked super attractive and somehow vulnerable, and he loved the appearance and the smoothness he felt when he touched her. If she let the hair grow back, he couldn't believe the result would be nearly as attractive and appealing as her present hairless state. He had never seen another woman nude except in photographs, let alone made love to one. He had seen photographs of women with hair "down there" and thought it didn't look anywhere near as nice as Kate's bare look. Sometime, maybe, she could let it grow for comparison's sake, but she shouldn't be surprised or offended if he took one look and asked her to ply her razor. He admitted to being curious to see the alternative scenario but was sure he wouldn't like it nearly as much as the bare look he was already addicted to and, although he realized that shaving involved time and effort, he hoped she'd stay with it. Rather cheekily, he offered to give her support by his presence when she next had a shaving session.

She manoeuvred herself so that she could take the head of his penis into her mouth and sucked at it gently and lovingly for a while before lifting her head to look at his penis. Then, looking and sounding at first rather serious, she said, "I have always been determined that anyone making love to me would be circumcised like you have been. I knew I loved you, David, and I wanted so much to go to bed with you, hoping that you would be my first and only lover, but before we did so I needed to know you had been circumcised. I know circumcision, or the lack of it, in one's lover, one's future husband, may seem a trivial matter in comparison with all the other qualities one is looking for, but while nursing I have seen a lot of penises of all ages, some circumcised, but many more intact, and I do not like an uncircumcised penis at all. Even in a baby. With an adult, my feelings are much stronger. An intact penis doesn't look nearly as nice, is not as easy to clean and the foreskin looks untidy, gets wrinkly with age and sometimes can't be retracted fully or at all so that it can't be washed properly and is then a health hazard, sometimes even a menace, not only to its owner but also to his wife. A glans covered by a foreskin is in a perpetually moist environment and consequently prone to infection, while a foreskin can be a receptacle for debris. Compared with a circumcised penis, an intact one is unhygienic and therefore unhealthy as well as un-aesthetic and sexually I believe it doesn't perform as well. When looking after a patient, I sometimes have to pull back a foreskin to clean under it. When it's a baby or a small boy, it's not so bad - I just think it's something which shouldn't be there and he'd be better off without it – but when it's an adult I don't like it at all, because the area below the glans is like a waste trap and gets very smelly unless the owner washes himself carefully and frequently, and many don't. Even if I loved him, making love with someone who wasn't circumcised is, honestly, for me unthinkable - I just would not be physically or mentally able to take an uncircumcised penis into my vagina or my mouth. Sorry for going on like this, but I do want you to know why I feel so strongly about circumcision."

Kate had observed that David's erection had wilted during her homily, but his penis stiffened as she reached for it and continued, "That's why I needed to know that you had been circumcised and, what's more, done properly. I love this penis of yours, darling. During this last week since I first saw it, your penis with its permanently bare head and no surplus skin has given me so many wonderful erotic thoughts, thoughts which recur when I'm in bed or free to daydream – and I've done a lot of that on your account during the last week. Thinking of it entering my vagina with the glans completely exposed excites me. I love to think of it inside my vagina with the bare glans moving up and down and pressing against my vaginal wall as it transmits the exquisite pleasure you give me after you enter me. I love thinking of that bare head inside my mouth and reacting to my tongue as I lap at it. I love thinking of it clasped gently in my hand. I love the notion that, erect or not, it always looks ready to make love to me. Several times during the last week I have thought how fortunate I am that when you were a tiny baby your mother had you prepared for your future sex life – and, although she didn't know it, for me! – by having you circumcised and making sure that the operation was performed by someone who could achieve such a perfect result with just the right amount of skin removed to denude that beautiful glans of yours completely and leave just enough skin to cover the shaft with nothing to spare. I realize that your mother, like every other mother who recognizes the long term benefits that a circumcision confers, would have had to steel herself against the pain she knew you would suffer when it was done, and I know it's a selfish thought but I'm glad she had the necessary resolve, because for me your penis looks and feels perfect. After saying all that, I hope you won't think I love only your penis. I do love it but only as part of you, the person that I love. Mind you, a vital part! And I'm so happy, darling – you are a wonderful lover for me and I love you as I know you love me."

Lying there with Kate in his arms, David kissed her passionately before telling her that the last week had been the happiest of his life. He loved her, and she had made him enormously happy. He had fallen in love with her very soon after they had first met and he wanted to spend the rest of his life with her and try to make her as happy as she had made him. After he thought about the implications of the question she asked him in the tea room, he had realized that she was as serious about their relationship as he was and saw them as having a future together. But he had continued to think she was nowhere near ready to go to bed with him. He had not connected last week's invitation to spend the day with her at her house with the question she had asked and he had been stunned – in a delightful way – when he arrived to be invited to share a bath with her. It was the best thing that had ever happened to him. They had come a long way very quickly, he was very, very happy and hoped she hadn't felt pressured by him into doing anything which she would rather not have done. Kate was emphatic that she was glad, very glad, that she had given him her virginity. She had made her own decisions and was extremely happy with the way things had turned out. "I do love you, David, and I hope now more than ever that we will get married and spend the rest of our lives together. The two days we've been together make me more than ever confident that you are the man for me." David told her that he loved her more now than ever, valued what she had given up to him and knew that marrying her was the thing he most wanted.

As they lay there in bed, Kate told him about her visit to Margaret and how shrewd and accurate her analysis of his penile status had been. She also told him about the common room debate and the contributions by Jenny and Trish, which made them both laugh. Kate said she hoped he wouldn't think she was unhinged about wanting a circumcised lover and husband, but it was important to her, aesthetically and sexually, as well as hygienically. David said that on the contrary, he was flattered that she liked his being circumcised – he'd always been glad he'd been done, but didn't know that girls cared one way or the other. He told her that if he hadn't been done and she had asked him to have the op, he would have agreed, of course, but he would have been in a quandary as to how to go about arranging it. He wouldn't have liked to ask his mother's help – she had always been completely open with him about sex, but she would undoubtedly have been curious about his motives and, anyway, if he hadn't been circumcised it would have been because she, a doctor as well as his parent, had decided against having him circumcised and his wanting a circumcision would have implied that he thought her earlier decision was wrong and might hurt her feelings, professionally as well as personally. He supposed he would have asked Kate to use her contacts to find out how to get it done.

Then he asked her, "Tell me, Kate, if I had told you in the tea room that I hadn't been circumcised, how would you have reacted? What would you have done? Would you have asked me there and then to have the op or would you have waited and raised the matter in more intimate surroundings?" "I'm a tougher cookie than most people think," said Kate, "and, yes, I would certainly have asked you then and there. I had made up my mind to do that when I decided to ask you whether you had been circumcised. Although I realize it's a big thing to ask a man, I knew you quite well enough to be sure you would have the op if I asked you and, more importantly, not resent being asked to have it. I know that sounds arrogant, but you love me, David, and you know I love you, and I was certain that once you knew that having a circumcised lover was important to me you wouldn't be deterred by fear of pain or anything like that from getting it done and arranging it without delay. We're both mentally tough people and I knew that if I made that request I would leave the tea room with an affirmative answer. I can't say I would have been entirely happy, because I would have been thinking it was going to be an ordeal for you and that I was the cause of it. But I had made up my mind to ask you in the tea room to have a circumcision if you hadn't already been circumcised. I was delighted when you told me you had been circumcised, both for the fact itself and out of sheer relief that I didn't have to ask you to get it done."

She hesitated for a moment, then she said, "In the tea room I asked you only if you had been circumcised. I would have liked to ask you also if you had had a full circumcision, that is one in which the glans is always completely bare, even when you are not erect. I hoped that you would have had a full circumcision but I felt I couldn't ask that second question there and then – it would have been a question too many in that tea room. Last week when we were in the bath, if it had turned out that you had an incomplete circumcision, it wouldn't have stopped me from making love with you but I would have asked you to get it corrected before we married as it is very important to me that my husband – my lover – should have a glans which is completely and permanently bare. Thank goodness your circumcision was done properly and completely – not all are."

Kate turned towards the innocent cause of her former concerns both now happily resolved. She caressed the glans before taking it in her mouth. David found the sensations caused by Kate's mouth and the movements of her lips and tongue on the head and upper part of the shaft of his penis and her manually caressing the skin covering the lower part of the shaft almost unbearably stimulating, but Kate wasn't yet sure whether to prepare his penis for reception in her vagina or try for the first time to bring him to orgasm in her mouth. She realized how adventurous she was becoming. If she brought him to climax in her mouth she wasn't sure if she would be able to bring herself to swallow the ejaculate – she knew some girls did, but others said it made them gag. She played for time while she made up her mind by taking his engorged organ out of her mouth and holding it gently in her hand, saying to him, "I love having you in my mouth, but I don't think I could take a penis normally covered with a foreskin into my mouth, even if it was fully retracted and clean – it just wouldn't seem hygienic. But yours has this lovely bare head that's permanently bare and absolutely no surplus skin on the shaft and I love it that way whether it's in my vagina or my mouth." Putting her thoughts into words helped solve her immediate dilemma. "Well," she said to herself, "let's just see how it goes!" and she asked David if he would like her to suck him off, explaining that he'd have to be patient with her as she would only have her instincts to guide her this first time. The idea of Kate using her mouth to bring him to orgasm excited David still further and made him rampant. Then he remembered how much they had both enjoyed his using his mouth and tongue to pleasure her while she lay across the bed on her back and he knelt on the floor between her parted legs. The thought thrilled him so he asked her if she would mind if he sat on the bed with her kneeling on the floor facing him while she brought him off. Kate, equally excited by the idea, readily assented.

Kate got up from the bed and John swung his legs over the side of the bed and moved into a sitting position as she knelt between his legs. She leaned forward and took his very excited penis into her hand, telling him to be sure to tell her if she was hurting him or not giving him as much pleasure as he thought she could do. Then she took his penis into her mouth again and experimented how far she should use the movement of her head and how to use her tongue and, more cautiously, her teeth to maximum effect. The groans coming from David were most encouraging, she considered – plainly her teeth weren't emasculating him – and she continued her efforts while trying to make up her mind whether to disengage when she judged he was on the brink of ejaculating – "cowardly," she thought – or take his semen in her mouth when he went off and swallow it if she found she could or spit it out on to a tissue. She thought – and this is the measure of Kate as a lover - that if she could take his semen in her mouth it would be more satisfying for both of them and still more satisfying if she could swallow it. So this very loving girl pressed on and when David came to a shuddering and noisy climax she took his ejaculate in her mouth, as near the front as she could manage, and, finding the salty taste not unpleasant, she summoned all her resolve and swallowed it. David recovered enough to thank her delightedly for the intense pleasure she had given him and said he hoped his penis tasted okay. "Sure," she said jauntily, "just one of the reasons why I wanted a circumcised lover!" He also thanked her for letting him go off in her mouth and asked if she'd had any trouble with swallowing his semen. "I didn't know what it would be like. I know some girls swallow it and some won't. But it didn't taste bad at all, a bit salty, and I did manage to swallow it, all of it, every last drop," she said proudly. "Now we'll find out if it's true that swallowing semen increases one's bust size – I can afford to make that experiment because I'm small up there!" Laughing as he spoke, David told her, "Don't you dare, Kate! Your breasts are perfect. They're very sexy just as they are. I don't want them any different - not even if you have to spit out my precious nutritious semen!"

Then she said, "Now it's my turn. You've kissed my vulva and licked me pretty thoroughly down there. Do you think you would like to bring me to orgasm with your mouth and tongue? I would love to try it. Some girls say it's even more satisfying than intercourse. I doubt that, but I'm sure it would give me lots of pleasure. This time will you do me that way, please, David? Please!" He kissed her by way of answer and got off the bed while she laid herself across the bed on her back and manoeuvred herself so that her bottom was on the edge of the bed and her feet resting on the floor. She opened her legs as wide as she could and when he knelt on the floor between them she brought her legs up and settled her thighs on his shoulders. Then she crossed her legs and used them to draw his head towards her. She grasped his head between her hands so that she could guide the movements of his mouth and tongue. She had no pubic hair for him to contend with, and he began using his tongue gently to caress the lovely soft skin covering her mons, her parted labia, the long slit of her vulva and, very, very gently the area around her clitoris. David thought how lovely she looked and tasted. She was moaning now and lifting her hips to increase the pressure on her of his tongue as it moved slowly from one part of her vulva to another. As he concentrated on the area adjacent to her clitoris, her excitement mounted towards climax and her soft moans increased in volume and frequency, her hips bucked more and more vigorously and she finally attained her orgasm quite noisily. Her movements stopped and she lay panting. After a while, she raised her head and smiled happily at him. David lifted her so that she was lying full length on the bed and lay beside her cuddling her until her breathing became more regular. She told him he had given her a marvellous orgasm and an experience that she would want to repeat very often in the future although nothing could ever wholly replace her pleasure in feeling his erect penis snug inside her. Though they both felt quite sleepy, they didn't dare go to sleep in case they overslept and were discovered in mid-slumber on her parents' return; after their exertions neither could summon the energy to get up and set the alarm on Kate's clock.

Soon it was time for a snack which they took in the nude in the kitchen. David sat on the old chair which had supported him as he deflowered his beloved only a week before and watched Kate as she moved about the kitchen preparing their light meal. How beautiful she looks and how gracefully she moves, he thought, and content to be observed; what a difference the last week had made to them – if there was any shyness between them now it was minimal. They were comfortable under each other's gaze and today had banished, largely at least, the taboo on bodily functions being observed in progress.

As intended, the snack revived them and they were glad to find their energies were not yet totally spent. As Kate put the mugs and plates in the sink she became aware that an erect penis was brushing her behind and hands fondling her breasts. He led her back to her bed. Both had heard of the 69 position and they decided it was time to try it. David, familiar now with the delights of that enticing region between Kate's legs, more or less dived for it and Kate, having literally acquired a taste for David's penis before lunch, took it in her mouth again without any hesitation at all. This time they bucked in unison as their passions mounted. Both were enjoying the position but Kate, thinking that David must be reaching the limits of his sexual endurance and wanting to feel his penis inside her for one last orgasm that day, lifted her head from her exertions and his erection and asked that he enter her vagina – actually that was what she intended to say but, and again it shows how far her former modesty had deserted her as a result of two days vigorous and wholly enjoyable sexual activity, she was slightly shocked to hear herself say, "David, darling, let's fuck; I want to feel that big hard cock of yours where it belongs in my vagina." They shifted position and she unrolled another condom on to his penis, then Kate turned on to her back and, opening her legs to receive him, guided David's penis into her welcoming cleft.

They came, David first followed by Kate.

Afterwards she felt ashamed of the language she had used and said, "David, darling, I'm sorry about the language I used. I don't really approve of words like "fuck" and "cock" as I think they are often used in a demeaning sense. I was brought up always to use the proper technical words. But proper words like "intercourse" and "penis" are impersonal and at that moment, I suppose, I instinctively wanted to use words which weren't impersonal or elegant but would be expressive of the need I felt. I urgently wanted you to enter me and, yes, fuck me. I wanted you to thrust your lovely circumcised cock into me and thrust and thrust over and over again until we both went off into orgasms. There, now I hope you'll forgive me this time and whenever I get carried away by passion and use unladylike language in the face of my need for you! Am I forgiven?" She put her face up to him to be kissed, got a long, lingering kiss and was told that he not only forgave her but had been turned on even more than he already was by his realization of her excitement and her need to be "fucked" – her message had come over loud and clear and his reaction to what she had said was sheer joy that she so obviously wanted him. He positively wanted her to use that sort of language when her feelings led her to want to use it – not to suppress it. After all, they had agreed always to be frank with each other and if what she said wasn't frank he didn't know what was. And whenever he told her he wanted to fuck her he hoped she would understand the urgency of his situation, too!

They lay together in David's arms until he could no longer resist caressing her breasts and then teasing her nipples to erection before he rolled over and kissed each of her little rosebuds. Then it was time to get up, make the place shipshape and clear it of incriminating evidence (which included several used condoms, as well as David himself), before her parents' homecoming.

Chapter 8

Progress

Now that David and Kate had experienced the delights of full intimacy, it was apparent to them that they needed regular encounters with the assurance of complete privacy and could not rely on Kate's parents' rare absences from home during term time at her brothers' schools. They reviewed their options. Their budgets were, like most students', minimal, so any thought of going to a hotel was out of the question, even if their age didn't lead to embarrassing questions by staff when they booked in. David's mother had her surgery in her house, ran her medical practice from there and was rarely away from it for more than a couple of hours at a time and, worse than that, might return home at any time, so his parents' home offered the lovers no prospect at all for the freedom from interruption they required. Fortunately, both Kate and David had sympathetic friends – some being young nurses whom Kate knew and others acquaintances of David who were attending the university - living in small flats who would lend them the key during the day and during longer absences when they were away visiting their families during weekends or vacations.

Thanks, therefore, to their friends, as well as the very occasional availability of Kate's family home when her parents and brothers were away from home, she and David were able to spend time together without fear of interruption and took the fullest advantage of any opportunity which came their way. While never losing any of the awe and admiration each felt for the other's unclothed body, they were already becoming accustomed to seeing each other in the nude. David loved to see Kate's breasts freed from the bra and other apparel which hid them from the gaze of those less privileged than he and found the subtle movements of her breasts and buttocks enthralling as she walked around unclothed. She, for her part, liked to see him naked, too. David's penis and scrotum were not large – she assumed they were about average in size – and his testicles were not pendulous, but she thought how well formed he was and always got a surge of pleasure when she saw him moving around unclad, whether his penis was erect – "when duty calls" as she thought – or relaxed. When it was relaxed the glans was totally bare and the skin of the shaft smooth and unwrinkled, proving him to have the perfect circumcision she had hoped for in her lover. Kate was fascinated by the process of erection, the change in size of the penis and the speed with which it occurred. Her touching David's penis even gently, or sometimes his mere awareness of her presence, was enough to trigger an erection. She appreciated that if he had not been circumcised, the process of erection would have been visually more spectacular as the foreskin covering the penis retracted to reveal the glans hidden beneath the skin. But, as she told herself, she had no regrets about his circumcision, no regrets at all.

One opportunity for the use of a friend's flat came up when Kate was having a period. Her sexual desires did not disappear during a period. It was a situation she felt she should discuss with David before she accepted her friend's offer as she understood that many men were turned off by periods. David said that if she wanted to make love during her periods then they should try it out and see how they could adjust to it so that their needs were met. As it happened her flow was very light at the time the flat was available and, Kate having taken the precaution of again borrowing her mother's old towel to cover her friend's bed, they both enjoyed an afternoon's lovemaking with full intercourse in the flat.

During the earlier part of her periods when the flow was greater she thought full intercourse would be impracticable but that didn't stop them going to bed together even if it cramped their style somewhat. Some weeks after their tryst at Kate's friend's flat, the flat was lent to them again but this time Kate was experiencing a heavy flow as she had explained to David. They let themselves into the flat and spread the old towel over the under sheet of the bed before undressing. As usual this was a process they enjoyed, and as she removed his underpants she was glad to see that, even though she was keeping her panties on and he already knew that they wouldn't have intercourse, his penis had retained all its enthusiasm for her and was very erect.

She lay on the bed and as he approached she welcomed him with outstretched arms. He lay down beside her and they cuddled and kissed and he fondled her breasts. Knowing that intercourse was off the menu that day, his penis had subsided and was relaxed as it rarely was when they were together in bed. Kate, however, had plans for his penis – the fact that intercourse was out didn't mean that they couldn't have pleasure – and she raised herself on one elbow and took his penis in one hand so that she could study it. Using the forefinger of her other hand she lightly traced the line of his circumcision which was only very faintly visible, running in a straight line round the skin of the shaft of his penis just below the head of the penis. Her touch made his penis stir in her hand. She asked him, "Do you know how old you were when you were circumcised, darling?" He told her, "I think it was done when I was about two weeks old. Just before I started to board at my prep school, my mother was giving me a bath when she told me that when I was at school I would find that some boys had penises that looked different from mine. She explained that soon after I had been born and while she and I were still in the nursing home, she had arranged for me to have a minor operation in which the skin covering the end of my penis was cut away so that the head of my penis would be exposed. This was to make it easier to keep it clean. Mummy said that some boys had this operation, which she told me was called circumcision, done to them either because the skin couldn't be pulled back to allow the head to be washed or because their parents thought it was better to do it anyway. A boy who had not been circumcised still had a sleeve of skin called a foreskin covering the end of his penis. Mummy said she thought all boys should be circumcised, so she had arranged to have it done at the nursing home where I was born before she took me home." Kate responded, "I'm very glad, as you know, that you have been circumcised and pleased that your mother had it done so neatly. We can't make love today with you inside me unfortunately, but I've got a special treat in mind which I hope you will enjoy as much as I know I shall!" She reached over to her handbag which she had placed on the bedside table and extracted a small leather case which she opened. It was her manicure case and it contained a variety of instruments closely resembling surgical instruments, including nail files, scissors and tweezers, which she laid out on the bedside table. "Darling, I know you haven't got a foreskin, thank goodness, but I want you to pretend you have one and I'm going to pretend to circumcise you. I would like you to pretend that you are the week or two week old baby that you were when your mother had you circumcised and saved us both so much trauma later. I've seen quite a lot of circumcisions done, mostly babies, but several older boys from toddlers to teenagers and a few adults, so I know what happens!" They grinned at each other. David told her that if she could conjure up fantasies like this one to enliven her periods, they weren't going to be the drag he had feared and maybe she should think about having them twice a month or more often. His penis had become erect.

Kate got a small bowl of warm water and some soap and washed his penis carefully, making believe that she was trying to retract his non-existent foreskin as she washed him. Then she dabbed him dry. She told him that she would now be applying antiseptic solution to his penis. He was lying on his back with his head raised to watch her as she grasped the skin covering the shaft and tried to pull it forward over the rim of his glans, but failed due to the lack of skin. "Oh dear," she said, "we've got an awful lot of pretending to do here!" She took up the tweezers telling him they were the forceps with which she going to clamp his foreskin and use as a guide for cutting away the right amount of foreskin at an angle parallel to the base of his glans. Holding the forceps in her left hand, she picked up the nail file, telling him it was a scalpel, and proceeded to go through the motion of severing his foreskin using the outer edge of the forceps as a guide. Next, she passed the scalpel slowly round the rim of his glans, explaining that she was cutting away the remains of the inner layer of his foreskin, which would still be partially covering his glans, to ensure that the glans would be completely and permanently bared. Then she went through the motions of putting in stitches to hold the cut surfaces together and bandaging him before saying, "Now, my darling baby, you're circumcised and properly prepared to give pleasure in twenty or so years time to a randy girl called Kate who loves the sight of a tightly circumcised penis like you now have. End of fantasy – back to reality, darling. I love to feel how taut your skin is. There's no slack skin even when you aren't erect but when you are erect it's really taut on you. Your circumcision was very neatly done – it's fortunate for both of us that your mother got a real expert to circumcise you, dearest one. When you make love to me, I like to raise my head and look at your lovely penis as I'm guiding it towards my vagina and, as I do that, I love to pull back on the skin of the shaft of your penis so I both see and feel the bare glans and tightly stretched skin of your erect, circumcised penis as you enter my vagina. I love the feeling that bare-headed, circumcised penis gives me as you enter me, and I'm thinking how happy and grateful I am that you were circumcised, darling – circumcised for my benefit as well as yours. I feel very grateful to your mother – it's too bad I can't thank her for having her son circumcised! When we have a baby boy I shall be just like your mother in wanting to make sure that his glans is permanently bared as carefully as she made sure that yours was."

While she was speaking Kate was holding David's penis in her hand and the combined effect of her touch, the fantasy they had acted out and what she had said was to ensure that the penis in her hand was very erect indeed, so Kate leant over to kiss it. Then, allowing David to caress and kiss her breasts and lifting her head so that she could watch its gyrations, she massaged his penis to a full, shuddering orgasm.

Chapter 9

Engagement

Soon afterwards, David and Kate announced their engagement with the full approval of their families, both sets of parents being very happy with their child's choice of partner. David's only regret was that he couldn't afford to buy Kate as expensive an engagement ring as he would like to have got her, but Kate, being the type of girl she was, didn't mind the smallness of the diamond – being engaged was what mattered. It was understood that they wouldn't marry until David had qualified as a chartered accountant and Kate as a State Registered Nurse and they were in a position to support themselves. After some time had passed following their engagement and each set of parents had received satisfactory assurances from their own child about the use of contraception, their parents put no obstacle in the way of their sharing a bed when staying together at either family's home, except that it was understood that they would not sleep together at Kate's house when her brothers were there.

After David had spent a weekend with Kate at her parents' home, Mary was sounding Kate out on her wedding plans and took the opportunity of mentioning with studied casualness that before one of her own nursing colleagues had married her fiancé had been circumcised at her request. She looked keenly at Kate to see if this sparked a reaction but, having decided it would be more fun to put her mother on the spot, Kate did not rise to her mother's bait, saying only, "Oh, really. How enterprising of her!" After a short pause to recover from this piece of cheek, Mary realized a direct approach was going to be necessary and said, "Kate, since you and David became close I haven't said anything to you about this but as you know I've always been convinced that circumcision is beneficial not only to the man but also to his wife. I haven't asked you about David, but if he hasn't been circumcised, have you considered asking him to have it done?" Knowing her mother as well as she did, Kate had been certain that she would be asked about David's penile status sooner or later and had been looking forward to a golden opportunity of teasing her mother when she did ask. She smiled inwardly. "Gosh, Mum, how should I know? How on earth would one go about asking such a very personal question? Or making such a request? I'd be much too shy." Mary was not deceived by the innocent expression Kate had assumed for her mother's benefit. She said, "I wasn't born yesterday, young lady. Nor were you. You've been sleeping with him and you haven't just been reading Peter Rabbit stories to each other before you nod off. Come on, Kate!" Kate's response was indignant. "I'm very shocked, Mum, that it's taken you so long to ask and that you risked my health by giving us permission to share my bedroom without asking him first. If it was my daughter I would have asked any suitor of hers before assenting to her becoming engaged – no, even before I allowed them to date - "Young man, have you been circumcised? No? Indeed, how very remiss of your mother. Well, don't call on my daughter until you can produce a medical certificate signed by the surgeon." I hope you don't think that a daughter brought up by you would be so unfilial as to sleep with an intact male. Of course he's been circumcised." Then she spoiled her show of indignation by giggling. Her mother laughed. "I was sure I could rely on you, Kate. Anyway, I've always liked his mother and was certain I could trust her to have seen to the matter, but it's just as well to make doubly sure, isn't it, dear?"

David had completed the full time component of his national service in the Royal Air Force between leaving school and going to university and, to fulfil his reserve service commitment and at the same time earn some money, he had joined a reserve unit which gave him the opportunity of attending additional training courses during university vacations. He received service pay while on courses and this supplemented the allowance he received from his parents, so that occasionally while he was on a course and Kate had leave due, they were able to spend time together away from their homes staying at a hotel near the air force station where the course was being held.

The first time they did this was not long after their engagement was announced. David was scheduled to take a three week course and Kate was able to spend a week with him. They stayed at a small hotel close by the R.A.F. station to which David had been posted.

David had started his course before Kate could join him and he moved his kit from the Mess to the hotel on the Friday when Kate arrived. David met her on her arrival at the railway station. In honour of the occasion, Kate wore a wedding ring as well as her engagement ring, giggling as she put it on in the taxi en route to the hotel, where, with studied nonchalance, they booked in as man and wife. When they got to the door of their room and unlocked it there was no one about so David picked Kate up and ceremonially carried her over the threshold and deposited her on the double bed he had specified for their stay. He brought their bags into the room and latched the door before diving on to the bed to kiss Kate. As he lay beside her, they rejoiced in the fact that they would have more time together in the next nine days than they had ever had and as David was not on duty until Monday, they had over sixty hours of opportunity ahead of them that first weekend, interrupted only by the need to eat occasionally and to sleep.

Kate said she felt the need to freshen up after her train journey and she would like a shower before they made love. David asked if he could join her. He had been careful to book a room with its own bathroom. They stood by the bed undressing each other with the same excitement and pleasure as they had experienced on that first occasion at Kate's home. Fully disrobed, they stood locked in each other's arms and Kate was very conscious of the firmness of his erection against her body. He led her into the bathroom and turned on the shower, carefully adjusting the temperature of the water before Kate stepped into the shower cabinet, luckily a reasonably commodious one ("Built for two," remarked Kate), followed by David.

David stood behind Kate under the shower and, reaching round her, cupped her breasts with his hands and pulled their bodies together so that she could feel his very erect penis in the cleft between her buttocks. She moved her feet further apart and reached behind her to grasp his penis and steered it between her legs so that she could feel the sensation of the glans in contact with the lips of her vulva, a process which David, taller than her, aided by bending his knees to bring his penis lower. She greatly enjoyed the pressure of his penis against her sensitive parts and so did he, but it wasn't a position that he could sustain for very long on the slippery floor and he had to withdraw. He straightened himself to his full height and she turned towards him so that he could soap her breasts, tummy, upper thighs and the area between them while she washed his penis and scrotal sac before they rinsed themselves under the showerhead. Then they stepped out of the shower and dried each other with the large fluffy towels provided by the hotel. They were taking full advantage of the sensual opportunities of showering and drying with body contacts that increased the excitement and anticipation both had felt since arriving at the hotel. As they dried each other, David asked Kate if she would mind making love standing up, something they hadn't yet attempted. He said that he had wanted to enter her there and then in the shower, but had been afraid the floor of the shower cabinet might have been too slippery to give them a safe footing and the fact that he was taller than her might have made it difficult; also he thought it might be easier if the first time they did it they faced each other and, besides, he didn't like to try it without first being sure it was something she would like to do. Kate answered that she would love to try it – the idea really excited her, she admitted – and during the next week they would have lots of time to experiment to find ways of making love new to them. "Yes," she said, "do let's try it standing up. Let's put those telephone directories on the floor a foot apart by the wall over there so I can stand with one foot on each to make up for the fact you're taller than me and I'll lean against the wall for support."

Kate stood on the phone books and David stood between the two books. She was well lubricated and didn't need any jelly and David very erect indeed, so she guided him into her very easily and they began to make love, he caressing her breasts and each kissing the other deeply. Then an idea occurred to Kate, who withdrew her tongue from his mouth to ask him if she could try to wrap her legs around his waist while he supported her. With his hands under her bottom, she managed to lever herself against the wall as she brought first one leg and then the other around him to clasp him to her and what had been an enjoyable way of making love was transformed into what both agreed afterwards had been a really memorable act of love. Both reached extremely satisfying orgasms. Another good thing was that the exertion had made them sweat to the point that they now had an excellent excuse for another enjoyable shower before they went down for dinner. Before going down, they remembered to replace the phone directories where they had found them in case the chambermaid came into their room to turn down the bed while they were at dinner.

This was the first meal they took as an ostensibly married couple and Kate took private pleasure in being addressed by the waitress as a married woman. The food was nicely prepared and pleasantly served but they did not linger over the coffee. That comfortable double bed upstairs beckoned. They left the dining room as soon as decorum allowed and once back in their room, shed their clothes and were lying in bed in each other's arms very quickly indeed.

Kate told David that she had enjoyed making love standing up very much indeed and they agreed to put it on their list of approved positions. He asked her if there were any other positions she would like to try. Both had read several of the sex manuals then available – all had titles indicating that they were intended for married couples only although their readership was almost exclusively unmarried – and between them they thought of several worth trying. Both admitted they liked the missionary position they had used exclusively until that evening – they both thought that each being able to kiss the other's mouth and his being able to kiss her breasts during intercourse made it better than other positions and Kate said she would like to experiment with the missionary position by trying it without a pillow under her hips and varying the number of pillows so as to alter the angle of penetration to see which angle gave her the most stimulation. They agreed they would try the side by side position. Spurred by what had happened in the shower which he had found exciting, David asked Kate if she would be prepared to try the rear entry position with her kneeling on all fours and she agreed to give it a go. They also discussed the 69 position which they already used for foreplay and found a good preliminary to intercourse, and agreed that they would try it out not as a mere starter but as a main course.

As they discussed the pros and cons of the various positions they had read about or heard of, David was kissing Kate's breasts and teasing her nipples into erection as his finger gently caressed her vulva, while she had encircled his penis with her finger and thumb just below the glans and was delicately tugging downwards the skin of his shaft. The sensations each was inducing in the other called for immediate action and led to the flow of ideas about new positions coming to a stop and to David rolling her on to her back. She responded by opening her thighs and pulling him above her. They kissed deeply and, although he had a very full erection by now, she pulled the skin covering his shaft gently downwards with one hand while with the other, she guided him into her vagina, exclaiming as she felt his penis enter fully, "Oh, darling, I can feel my vagina is full of penis and it feels so good. I wanted you in there so much. Do me, darling, please do me, and make me come." She moaned as he moved rhythmically within her and she moved in harmony with him. He climaxed first and she thought this triggered her own orgasm which she was sure was the most powerful she had yet experienced. Afterwards, feeling drained but very happy, she lay still for a while before saying, "Tonight has been the start of a wonderful week together. Thanks for being such a considerate lover, darling. I hope I can make you as happy as you make me." He told her he was the happiest man alive and hoped that he could keep her happy for the rest of their lives. Wrapped in each other's arms and thinking happily about the week that lay ahead of them, they kissed for a while before sleep overtook them.

During Kate's stay, David had to spend normal working hours from Monday to Friday at the R.A.F. station. They had an early breakfast together at the hotel each weekday morning before David left her and they met at the hotel after David's last lecture of the day. They were pleased to find that David was able to get back to their hotel with plenty of time for them to have a shower and a session in bed before having a latish dinner which energized them sufficiently for more pleasure before they slept.

After David's return one day to the hotel, they were in the shower cubicle and he was standing behind her soaping her back and thighs and marvelling as he always did at how beautiful her body was. He reached around her to take her breasts in his hands and caress them. He began to soap them, feeling her nipples harden as he did so. His penis was erect, of course, and she was standing with her legs far enough apart for him to be able to flex his knees and, using his hand, to guide his penis between her legs. Kate gasped and turned her head to kiss him. It was a lovely sensation for both of them – Kate could feel the head and shaft of his penis pressing upwards along the whole length of her vulva, whose outer lips had parted with the excitement she felt and the head was exerting gentle pressure on her clitoris and he could feel her returning the pressure on the dorsal side of his penis from tip to root. It felt lovely but, as they knew from a previous occasion, it was not a position he could maintain and as he reluctantly withdrew his penis he plucked up his courage to ask her if they could go to bed and do it "doggie-style" as they knew this so far untried position was called. "Yes, let's," responded Kate, "but you know I'm not at all keen on the idea of anal intercourse, so don't get carried away before I navigate you into the right entrance, will you?"

They dried off quickly. Standing by the bed they kissed deeply before Kate sat on the edge of the bed and laid her upper body backwards on the bed so that David could kneel between her thighs and kiss and caress her to bring her to a high level of excitement. Then she delved into the bedside cabinet for the surgical jelly and, although already well lubricated by her own secretions, smeared a coating on the entrance to her vagina and, for good measure, the head of his penis.

Kate pulled the bedclothes down, positioned a towel on the bed and climbed on to the bed, putting her head on the pillow and knelt on all fours with her knees well apart. Standing by the side of the bed, as she positioned herself, David thought how truly beautiful she looked, completely nude and kneeling as she waited for him, her body a series of sensuous, lovely curves. He got on the bed and knelt between her legs with a view of her beautiful bottom positioned most provocatively, aware that she was awaiting his entering her. It was immensely exciting and as he moved forward, her left hand clasped his erect penis just below the head and, encircling the shaft, eased the glans into position at the entrance of her vagina, then, slipping down the shaft, guided the rest of his penis into her waiting vagina. To begin with, both moved their bodies very gently and tentatively, each trying to ensure the other's comfort and gauging how the other liked this new found position. Soon both had the confidence to increase the tempo of their movements and to thrust towards the other, mirroring the pleasure each now felt sure the other was communicating. Both reached orgasm and slowly allowed their movements to subside. With Kate's consent David withdrew his penis and they lay side by side, each facing the other, David kissing her and fondling her breasts. He asked her if she had enjoyed it and she said she had – very much – but commented that although he had been able to caress her breasts he couldn't kiss either her breasts or her mouth nor could she kiss him, and she missed all that. On the whole, they agreed, they preferred the missionary position but this new way was one they should use quite often as it certainly had given them both some new and enhanced sensations.

Throughout that week, Kate was the delightful companion full of fun and surprises that David had come to find her. On his return to the hotel from his day with the air force, they often tumbled into bed and stayed there, only dragging themselves out to eat dinner just before the dining room closed. One evening on his return to the hotel, Kate asked him with a mischievous smile, "Do you know what I am?" "An engaged woman and a nurse – good-looking and very bed worthy, too," he replied, slightly puzzled by the question. Kate responded, "I'm all of those, I hope, and an acucullophiliac as well." "What on earth's that?" enquired David. She explained, looking even more mischievous, "I was reading a women's magazine in the hotel lounge and in the agony column there was an item about acucullophilia which was defined alternatively as "attraction to men who are circumcised" or "the condition of being sexually aroused only by circumcised males." I qualify under both definitions, but it's alright – it's not certifiable." She laughed happily and so did he. "I always knew I was born under a lucky star. First, my mother has me circumcised and then I fall in love with a beautiful girl whose mother has brought her up as an acucullophiliac! What more could a man want?" asked he. "Except this, of course," he added grabbing her and steering her towards the bed from which they emerged only just in time for a very late dinner.

Another day they took a bath together before dinner. David got into the bath before Kate and was lying full length in it when Kate entered the bathroom. The first thing she observed was his penis awash on the surface of the bath water like the periscope of a submerged submarine. She seized it with a joyful whoop and began to wash it with all the fervour a nurse can summon up in the cause of hygiene – the process being much enjoyed by patient and nurse alike. Then she stepped into the bath and they knelt facing each other while they soaped and rinsed each other. While so engaged, David asked Kate if she would mind their having a 69 session all the way to climax instead of limiting it to foreplay. Kate agreed they should try it out – with a lifetime ahead of them they should experiment with as many themes as possible and those they liked they should make a regular part of their life together.

They stepped out of the bath together and dried each other

with the big fluffy towels the hotel changed each day. Then they pulled the bedclothes down and Kate put a towel over the under sheet "in case of accident," she said.

Kate lay on the bed with her head on a pillow placed about half way down the bed with her head and upper body positioned as if she was lying on her side but her hips and legs were flat on the bed and her feet extended beyond the low foot board. David climbed on the bed and lay on his side parallel to her but with his feet at the headboard end and his head so placed that he could kiss the area between her legs while his penis was close to her mouth. David caressed her breasts and as her nipples hardened he moved so that he could kiss them and left a trail of kisses down her torso to her flat tummy and down her thigh nearest to him and then, as she parted her legs, slowly back up the inner side of her thigh to the immaculately shaven area of her vulva. Her growing excitement had already caused the lips of her labia to part, and they parted further as his tongue probed gently between them and in the region of her clitoris. He was conscious that she was already very wet and she was moaning softly.

Meanwhile Kate's hand had gently encircled David's erect penis just below the glans and moved down his penis exerting on the skin covering the shaft just sufficient pressure to ensure that the skin was as taut as it could be without inflicting any pain. The effect was, as Kate intended, to give him an erection of maximum, almost unbearable, intensity. She moved her head so that she could use her tongue to follow the faint greyish, almost invisible, line running around his penis just below the rim of its head. He shuddered with pleasure and anticipation as he felt the progress of her tongue around this most sensitive part of his penis, determined not to give way to the urge to ejaculate which was already building powerfully within him. When Kate's tongue had completed its journey round his penis she took his totally bare and throbbing glans into her mouth and began to give it the most exquisite pleasure while he continued to deploy his tongue to excite her clitoris. Kate momentarily released his penis from her mouth and said, rather huskily, "Poor little wounded penis" before replacing it between her lips. David realized that she was thinking of his circumcision as a baby and was deeply touched that her pleasure that he had undergone the operation was tempered by her appreciation of the pain it would have caused him at the time. He disengaged his tongue from pleasuring her vulva just long enough to respond by saying, "You may be a raging acucullophiliac, but you're a wonderfully compassionate girl and I love you for it. Darling, we're both glad I was circumcised; it gives you pleasure and that gives me pleasure."

Then followed a period of intense mutual delight when each gave and received enormous pleasure. David was careful not to let his tongue press directly on the delicate tissues of Kate's clitoris in case he caused her discomfort and even pain, and he was watchful for any sign, however slight, that he was not giving her the full measure of pleasure he wanted her to have. Kate, for her part, was careful not to let her teeth engage too closely with David's penis. But, taking these precautions which each had already learned from the other, they were able to give each other a degree of pleasure which they agreed later was exquisite.

Finally David gave way to what had become an imperative need to ejaculate and Kate was ready to receive it when it came, warned by the increased throbbing of the organ in her mouth and the rising intensity of the groans of its owner. Kate herself had a series of orgasms. As they showered and dressed in time to be the last guests to enter the dining room, they agreed that it had been a most pleasurable way of showing their love for each other and one to revisit – often.

Another day they were emerging from the shower when David asked her to lie on her tummy on the bed and let him lie above her with his penis between her buttocks, not entering her as he knew that, like him, she was not keen on the idea of anal intercourse, but so that they could satisfy the curiosity both felt and had discussed about the sensations the position would give them. Kate readily agreed and lay face downwards on the bed with her hips on a pillow, her legs well apart. When David climbed above her and knelt between her thighs she brought her hand round her back to guide his erect penis to the entrance to her anus and held it there touching but not entering her for several minutes while she massaged his penis gently and then, feeling his rising excitement, guided his penis away from her anus to a position in the cleft between her buttocks where she brought him to orgasm manually. Afterwards he thanked her for trying it out, but both agreed that anal intercourse was not an item on the menu although they had enjoyed the limited experiment. Kate told David that she had liked feeling the movements of his penis between her buttocks and the gush of warm semen as he ejaculated while he cheerfully admitted to the pleasure he felt in exploring a taboo area and the excitement he felt as she stimulated him with her hand behind her back – "sort of remote control" he said.

Kate had to return home on the Sunday in time to report to the nursing school on Monday morning so she had booked to travel on an early afternoon train from the nearby railway station. She and David had agreed to make the most of their time together on Sunday by having an early breakfast and returning to bed until they had to get up and vacate their room at the 12 o'clock checking out time.

Early on the Sunday morning Kate had awoken feeling uncomfortable. She quickly realized that she was starting her period earlier than she had expected and that the flow was a heavy one which was going to put an unwelcome crimp into their plans for the morning.

When David woke, she explained what had happened. After breakfast they returned to their room and as they packed, Kate said that although it wouldn't be practicable to have the super-active final session they had been looking forward to, there was no reason why they couldn't go back to bed together and pleasure each other. She would have to keep her tampon in place and her panties on but she always enjoyed being kissed and caressed and her breasts always enjoyed his attentions and she hoped that she would be able to satisfy him. It would be an opportunity for them to spend time together, even though there would be less activity than she had hoped.

As she spoke she was already undressing and putting on the

romantic, flimsy nightdress that she had brought with her but had never been given the opportunity to put on even briefly, let alone wear, during the past week. This was her chance to find out what it felt like to have one's nightie removed by one's lover, she thought. She climbed into bed and sat demurely as he undressed. As he slipped his pants off, she noted happily that her period had not deterred him from sporting his usual enthusiastic erection. He got into bed with her and they lay for a while, kissing deeply, while he fondled her breasts and she held his erection in her hand. He told her that she looked stunning in her nightie but in bed he much preferred her nude and asked if she would sit up so that he could have the pleasure of removing it. "After all," he said, "a nightie doesn't keep you warm. It has to be the only garment designed to give pleasure when seen and, after a brief viewing period, greater pleasure when being removed, followed by the greatest pleasure after its removal." Kate duly sat up and he removed the delicate wispy lingerie carefully so as not to damage it. Then she excused herself and went into the bathroom, returning with a small bowl of warm water, soap, a face cloth, two towels and a beaming, somewhat impish, smile and announced that since she was going back to being a nurse tomorrow she wanted to make sure that she hadn't forgotten how to give a bed bath and she hoped he would co-operate in this. He knew Kate well enough to know that whatever she was up to – and he knew from that smile that something was afoot - he was going to enjoy it, so he let her pull the bedclothes back and slip one of the towels under him as he lay there.

Kate knelt by the bed and took his erect penis in her left hand and exerted gentle pressure on the shaft to draw the thin skin covering it downwards so that she could wash his penis which she then dabbed dry with the other towel. She asked him if he would be embarrassed by her examining his penis very closely – his penis was something very important to both of them and with her temporarily out of action this was an opportunity for her to get to know it more intimately than she might otherwise ever achieve. She told him that ever since she had been a child the fact that some boys were circumcised had fascinated her. She told him about the circumcisions of Joan's baby and her own brothers and her mother's comments in answer to her questions. She said he knew how relieved she had been to discover that he had been circumcised. She had also been delighted and moved to know that he would have been prepared to undergo a circumcision for her sake if he hadn't already been circumcised. He knew she was an acucullophiliac, but she hoped he wouldn't think she was a crank about circumcision - she believed that it improved the hygiene of both the man and the woman he made love to, it lessened the incidence of malignant disease in both sexes, it improved the appearance of the penis and, best of all, through its reducing the sensitivity of the penis (so delaying the man's orgasm) it gave them both the chance of greater sexual satisfaction.

"You have what is to me a perfect penis. The head has a much greater circumference than the shaft and, due to the skill and good judgement of the surgeon who circumcised you and removed exactly the right amount of skin, you have no surplus skin at all, yet no problem in attaining full erection without discomfort. Thanks to the decision of your parents to have you circumcised and the surgeon who did it, I get a great big thrill every time I see you in the nude with your lovely bare glans."

As Kate spoke, she traced with the tip of her forefinger the faint, greyish, white line which marked where the cut edges of his foreskin had healed together in a straight line immediately below his glans. "It was really very skilfully done indeed," she said happily. "I wonder what method was used on you. The Jewish ones are often the best, even though a lot of the mohels are not surgeons or even doctors. There's one in town who's a chartered accountant – that's a thought, darling, after you qualify as a C.A. you could convert and moonlight as a mohel! A mohel uses a scalpel and a shield to protect the glans and doesn't put in stitches. They are carefully trained and expected to do the whole operation in about two minutes flat – much quicker and easier on the baby than a circumcision in a hospital. They operate in the presence of an audience of parents, relatives and friends which gives them an extra incentive to do it well and quickly. Some mohels will take on non-Jewish cases. Some non-Jewish doctors use variations of the Jewish ritual operation but substitute a pair of forceps for the shield and they usually put in stitches. Other doctors use special clamps to stop any bleeding – one is American and called the Gomco clamp. Another method, very new, is the Plasti-bell where the doctor makes a dorsal slit in the foreskin and pushes a plastic bell over the glans, pulls the foreskin back up over the bell and ties a nylon ligature round a groove at the base of the bell. This cuts off the supply of blood to the part of the foreskin above the ligature so that the skin falls off after three or four days. I've seen all these methods used and I think a mohel is generally better than even the best surgeon. Best of all, perhaps, is a Jewish doctor who taken the course to become a mohel."

Then she said huskily, almost whispering, "David, darling, have you ever imagined what it would have been like if you hadn't been circumcised as a baby and when I asked you in the tea house if you had been circumcised you had told me that you hadn't been circumcised? You know that I would have asked you to have a circumcision and you have told me that you would have had it done. But how would you have felt about it?"

David replied that he would positively have wanted to have it done because he realized it was important to her happiness and, therefore, to their future happiness as a couple and because he agreed with Kate that it was a beneficial health measure for both of them. Furthermore, he would have felt that if she was prepared to give him her virginity he should make some reciprocal sacrifice and giving her his foreskin seemed like an appropriate exchange for her hymen!

Then an idea came to him and he asked her if she would mind fantasizing with him what his adult circumcision would have been like if post tea house he had had the operation. "Oh yes," said Kate, "now that would be fun! Just the thing to dispel any gloom my wretched premature period has caused us! Let's go. I suppose you wouldn't have talked to your parents about it and you would have wanted me to use my medical and nursing and hospital contacts – fair enough, since I was, after all, the cause of the problem! I would have had to find a surgeon who could be relied upon to do a really neat job on you and to make an appointment for day surgery at the Royal Infirmary. You know my friend Margaret, who edited the nursing school gazette before me, is a theatre nurse in the minor surgery unit and I would have roped her in to help – she knew about you, remember! There's a surgeon called Wilson whom both Margaret and I have assisted at circumcisions of adults and adolescents as well as newborns and he's very, very good, so I would have asked him. I know that Margaret would have been able to cut the red tape in getting a minor surgery theatre booking and, very important this, getting me on the roster of assistants for the occasion.

"On arrival at the Infirmary, you would have had to book in at the admissions desk where I would have met you and then taken you to the private room booked through Mr. Wilson for you. There I would have left you while you undressed, put on one of those awful skimpy hospital gowns and got into bed. Margaret would have arranged for me to prep you and not have any other duties for the rest of the day. So when you were in bed I would have come back to you. Remember that I would never have seen you undressed before and it would have been a dramatic moment for both of us when I entered your room to prep you for the circumcision I had asked you to have done for my sake. You would have been nervous and I would have been worried about you, but excited too - very excited! I expect that we would have kissed and cuddled for a while before I pulled the blanket down and raised your hospital gown. You might have been apprehensive about the surgery to come but, knowing you as I do now, darling, my bet is that I would have been faced with a raging erection. So that you might have looked at that moment very much like what I'm looking at now. Anyway, I'm sure that if you weren't erect at that instant of revelation you would have become erect while I was prepping you because I would have to wash your penis and scrotum very thoroughly and I defy any man in love not to go very rigid indeed while that's being done to him by the object of his affections. For my part I would have been fascinated by my first sight of your equipment and, nursing ethics notwithstanding, I would have had to explore it. Actually, bringing you to orgasm would have relaxed you mentally as well as physically and that would make the operation less stressful for you. So I would have had a perfectly good excuse, although Matron might not have agreed. I would have washed you and then brought you by hand to a climax before I shaved you. I would have been grateful to have the opportunity to see your uncircumcised penis before it was altered forever and, although as you know I very much prefer the circumcised state, I would have greatly enjoyed my first and last opportunity of manipulating your intact foreskin and bringing you to orgasm. After you ejaculated and your erection subsided I would have washed you again and in doing so I would have retracted your foreskin right back, enabling me to show you what your circumcised penis would soon look like. Then I would have shaved your genital area before going to get Margaret who, as nurse in charge of a student nurse, would have had to pass you as properly prepared for the operating theatre. That's another reason why I would have wanted to give you an orgasm; when I brought her in – and you yourself have remarked what a good-looking girl she is – I wouldn't have wanted you to get an erection while she was checking my handiwork. She would have teased me mercilessly and made jokes about infidelity for the rest of my days!

"Then it would be off to the minor surgery theatre – not that you'd say it was minor surgery! – with you on a trolley and Margaret and me walking with you. I would have wanted very much to hold your hand as we went, but I wouldn't have been able to in the circs. Sorry, no pun intended. When I had asked Mr. Wilson to perform a circumcision on you I would have explained, of course, that you were my boyfriend and I would also have asked him to give you a nice, tight circumcision and remove your frenulum, the band of tissue which connects the head of the penis to the shaft. When we got to the theatre you'd have been transferred to the operating table and been draped and

Margaret (or me, if she had allowed me, and I'm sure she would have let me) would have daubed your genital region with an antiseptic. Mr. Wilson would give you a local anaesthetic by injecting you near the base of your penis and, after waiting for that to take effect, he would do a series of injections into the foreskin forming a ring right round your penis just below the part of the skin to be excised. Once he had satisfied himself that the injections had taken effect and your penis was fully anaesthetized, he would have made a dorsal slit cutting through your foreskin down the median from the top, here, to a point, there, just below the level of the corona – that's the rim – of your glans. Then he would trim away the two flaps of foreskin created by the dorsal slit, cutting away enough skin to ensure that the head of your penis would be completely bare at all times, and after that he would stitch the cut edges together. He would also excise the frenulum, there, and put in stitches to bring the cut surfaces together. Finally he would apply more antiseptic and then Vaseline to stop the gauze dressing from sticking to the wound, and tell you it was all over. He would probably have made some crack about the need for patience before putting his craftsmanship to the test, perhaps telling me, as well as you, not to hurry! That would have made me blush and Margaret giggle. It wouldn't only have been you who would have been nervous before and during the operation. I would have been apprehensive as well – excited too, at what was being done to you because of me. Now I would have the neatly circumcised lover of my dreams, and not many girls – even nurses – can say this, circumcised at my request and in my presence, too!

"Then you would be put back on the trolley and wheeled back to your room to recover for a couple of hours. The local anaesthetic would wear off and you would begin to feel some discomfort, but I would be sitting with you and as soon as that happened I would go and get Margaret to give you some painkillers. When you felt well enough, you would be able to leave hospital and I would have taken you home in a taxi, having first made sure that you were able to walk properly so that you wouldn't give yourself away the moment your mum saw you and recognized you as walking wounded. If no one was at home, I would have come in with you and tucked you up in bed before making myself very scarce quickly to ensure that you didn't have an erection and pop any of Mr. Wilson's stitches. Apart from dangling your pecker a couple of times daily in a glass containing warm water with cooking salt added for a few days to aid healing, that would have been that. Two weeks later – well, perhaps, to be on the safe side, three weeks – you would have been well enough healed to have made gentle love to me, but we would have had to wait a while longer until my parents had a day away before I could borrow the old kitchen chair and put your remodelled equipment to a real fitness test deflowering your virgin bride to be.

"Meanwhile I wonder what Margaret would have said to me when we next met. I know that she's happy that the chap she's engaged to is circumcised, but he was circumcised as a baby. She's a very nice girl and I bet she would have congratulated me on having a boyfriend who had demonstrated his love for me by going through the circumcision I had asked him to have for my sake, and she would have said she thought it very romantic and brave. That's just how I would have felt about you if you had been circumcised for me and I would have known I was a very lucky girl."

David's penis had felt sorry for itself during Kate's exposition of what might have happened to it and had wilted, despite her earlier praise of its appearance. So Kate addressed it, saying, "Poor thing, I've frightened it. That won't do at all." She grasped it gently and leant over him to take it into her mouth. Almost immediately it sprang to attention and Kate released it from her lips. Her fingers and thumb continued to grip it just below the glans and she began a rhythmical movement massaging the shaft quite vigorously. David moaned with pleasure as she manipulated him and he moved his hips in cadence with her massage of him. He wanted this state of bliss to go on forever but, greedy though he was, nature prevailed and after he called out to her "Darling, I'm coming," he ejaculated. Kate watched the several successive spurts emerge, gradually diminishing in force and volume, sharing and savouring his pleasure, even though she was thinking that had her period not started early she would have enjoyed receiving them deep within herself. She cleaned his penis with the face cloth and then, lying beside him, they remained in each other's arms, frequently kissing and occasionally fondling each other, he kissing and caressing her breasts and lightly touching her legs while she held his penis and gently played with it.

Eventually they had to get up for lunch and then go to the railway station where they parted after a really memorable week in which they had spent more time together and enjoyed more, and more diverse, couplings than ever before and confirmed more than ever their love and commitment to one another.

Chapter 10

Marriage

Several years had passed since David, then still a university student, had waved goodbye to his fiancée, Kate, as the train took her back home to continue her course at the nursing school at the end of their week together, while he was doing a training course with the R.A.F. during a university vacation. They had married after he had taken his degree, served his articles and qualified as a chartered accountant, and she had qualified as a State Registered Nurse. He was in practice in the firm of chartered accountants where he had articled and Kate was working, as she had always wished, as an operating theatre nurse at the Royal Infirmary. They were both doing well in their chosen careers and had bought a house.

Married life in no way staled the love of Kate and David for each other or dimmed the excitement that each felt whenever the opportunity for making love presented itself. Because Kate worked shifts on rotation at the Royal Infirmary, there were times when she got home much earlier than her husband and had time to prepare surprise encounters for him, like the day David returned home to find the house strangely silent and apparently deserted until he looked into their bedroom to find Kate, smiling beatifically, sitting up in bed in a glamorous nightie she had rarely been given the opportunity to wear, while on the bed lay an equally rarely used pair of his pyjamas, neatly pressed. Kate had carefully made herself up and explained that tonight she was the virgin bride who had not gone on honeymoon with him and he was this virgin bride's virgin bridegroom – "No experience required," she added kindly. She explained that she had been brought up strictly by very religious parents and taught in Sunday school. She was a student training to be an art teacher. Would he please understand that she was a shy, modest girl and be gentle with her as she was feeling quite frightened because of stories she had heard of men's wicked ways with maidens like her? Now, would he please remember his duty to his bride on this, their wedding night and get himself into the nice, warm bath that his loving bride had already prepared for him, but being so modest and shy did not think proper to share with him, and get out of it as quickly as decency and the demands of cleanliness made possible so that she could become a proper wife to him as soon as possible? After this speech Kate uncorked a bottle prominently labelled "Sal Volatile," sniffed at it delicately and fell back on her pillows in a swoon.

Faced with this call to duty, David gave his recumbent bride a chaste kiss on her forehead, picked up his pyjamas and, in short order, had his bath and returned to the bedroom clean and decent and clad in his pyjamas to find his bride had regained consciousness and was sitting up waiting for him. Doing his best to keep an unruly part of his anatomy imprisoned inside his pyjama trousers and determined to play the part of an eager but virgin bridegroom as well as he could, he climbed into bed beside his demure bride, put his arms around her and drew her towards him, making sure as he did so that her head and shoulders remained above his as he kissed her slowly and sensuously. Sure enough, as he had hoped, the flimsy nightdress proved even less able to contain her breasts than his pyjama trousers could conceal his erection, and a pert little breast soon came tumbling into view above him. He caressed it and kissed it and then, after pulling the thin shoulder straps of her nightie downwards off her shoulders, he began to kiss in turn both breasts in a series of concentric patterns ending by taking each tiny nipple into his mouth to tease it into erection with his tongue. Next, he eased the straps down her arms and released them so that he could feast his eyes on the whole upper half of her body. He was encouraged by the bride's lack of resistance so far, although he had heard a strangled whisper of "Mercy me!" as he had taken the first nipple into his mouth. Supporting her, he drew her downwards so that she was lying flat on the bed and continued to kiss her mouth and breasts and was relieved to find that she was returning his kisses with every sign of pleasure. Emboldened, he drew the bedding downwards so that the rest of her torso and the upper part of her legs were free of bedding and then, running his hand very gently downwards from her knee, he reached the hem of the long nightdress she was wearing. Once there he began to caress her leg, working his way upwards under her nightie past her knee onto her thigh and, pausing to look at her face, he saw that her lips were slightly parted and her eyes closed while she was breathing more quickly. Then he heard her low, urgent whisper "Please don't stop now!" So, very gently and slowly, he let his hand move towards her inner thigh and, as she parted her thighs to allow him access, upwards to her mons and then even more gently to the cleft of her vulva which he was further encouraged to find moist, very moist – indeed if he had not known her to have been a nervous virgin bride he would have said wet. He raised the skirt of her nightie to waist level to expose wholly her legs and her most intimate parts so that the nightie, lowered from the top and raised from below, now formed a wispy belt around her midriff. David, well aware as he was of Kate's loveliness when nude, tried to imagine himself as a virgin bridegroom seeing this El Dorado of beauty on his wedding night for the first time.

His thoughts were interrupted by his novice bed mate daringly extending an exploratory hand and finding an intriguing hard object contained within his pyjama trousers. He wasn't sure if this was in the script. Then, still more daringly, the virgin bride eased her find through the slit of his pyjama trousers and, with her other hand, undid the waist cord of his pyjama trousers and the buttons of his pyjama jacket. Still clutching her prize the brave girl tugged his trousers downwards so that he could kick them off while he slipped off the jacket. Both bride and bridegroom were now very satisfyingly free from encumbrances while each could see and feel the eagerness of the other to consummate their new union. The bride picked up the tube of surgical jelly that lay concealed on the bedside cabinet and, with a becoming touch of shyness, asked the bridegroom not to look and placed some jelly in the entrance to her vagina. This bride wanted to lose her virginity in the traditional position on her back with a pillow under her hips. As Kate opened her legs to receive him, she was holding his erect throbbing penis in her hand while happily pretending to herself that she had never previously seen nor been able to visualize the male organ until this evening of revelation. As soon as he had moved into position above her, she guided his penis into the entrance of what she thought of at that moment as her virgin vagina. True, there was insufficient hymen left to constitute any impediment but still Kate was able quite happily to imagine herself being deflowered again and took care to appear nervous as she navigated his penis past the remnants of her hymen, giving vent to a muted squawk at what she judged to be the moment at which her virgo ceased to be intacta. In complete harmony and with more skill than their novice characters could have mustered, Kate and David made love together and reached mutually satisfying climaxes.

Later, both completely spent, they lay together in bed, each with an arm around the other. The groom asked the bride solicitously if his breaking her hymen and entry into her vagina had hurt her and she was able to assure him with perfect truth that she had suffered no pain at all. Then David thanked Kate for thinking of the fantasy she had dreamed up, saying it had been great fun and an excellent excuse for making love at the end of the working day. Kate said it was an experience she had thoroughly enjoyed and further scripts were in preparation. They remained entwined in bed for a long while before they got up to enjoy the evening meal which Kate had prepared earlier and only needed warming up. After that they went back to bed as bride and bridegroom but, both being quite tired, went to sleep almost immediately.

The bridegroom woke quite early and as he needed to use the lavatory, got out of bed quietly so as not to disturb his bride and went into the bathroom. He was standing in front of the lavatory and was about to let fly when a voice behind him said softly, "I've always wondered how boys manage. Can I stay, please, and perhaps you can show me how to aim it?" He turned to kiss her and guided her hand to his penis which she grasped gently before he turned back and, after assuring himself that her aim was good, allowed himself to pee. After he finished, she continued to cradle his penis in her hand but he could see a puzzled look on her face and there was a pause, before in a low voice, she said, "Darling, down there you don't look like the male models who pose for us in the Art School. You don't have any skin over the end of your penis like all our models do. Yours looks nicer and neater. But why is it different?" She was still holding him as he explained that when he was a baby the skin covering the end of his penis had been cut away to expose the head in a minor operation called circumcision. "So that's what circumcision is!" exclaimed his bride, "I've heard about it in church – the Jews do it to their baby boys when they are a week old. And when our next door neighbour came with her baby to our house for coffee she told my mother that she was taking him to hospital the following week for his circumcision. After she'd gone I asked Mum what they were going to do to the baby, but all she would say was that it was an operation that little boys sometimes had. Typical! I wish parents would prepare their children properly for the real world. Last night, you know, I was frightened about what was going to happen when you made love to me. Mum had not told me and wouldn't answer my questions properly, telling me I should rely on you. Mind you, I knew that I could trust you. But what I didn't know was how wonderful it would be. And it was! Thank you, darling, for being so gentle with me and making our first night together such a lovely one, just perfect."

She picked up his face cloth, ran some warm water, soaped it and began gently to wash his penis, saying as she did, "So now I know what a circumcision is. Well, I must say that that I think your penis looks much better than the other kind and I'm delighted you were circumcised – it looks all the time as if you are ready to make love to me and I love that look. It's as if you were made ready to make love to me when you were a baby, and I find that a very erotic thought!" She dried him off with a towel and, still holding his penis, which by now her far from innocent attentions had brought to full erection, said, "We mustn't keep it waiting. Darling, will you make love to me before we go down for breakfast? We've got time." And she led him back to bed. Before getting into bed they stood kissing and he took off her nightie, which had remained draped around her waist through the night until she woke and put it back on before following him into the bathroom. As they stood there nude, he thought what a picture of sheer beauty she was and how well she had made the sudden transition from a chaste, modest, shy girl into an enthusiastic participant in lovemaking. Married life was wonderful! He lifted her light, lithe, lovely body gently and laid her on the bed. She held out her arms to him in an invitation to join her. For a while they lay kissing each other with increasing passion while he caressed her breasts and later her vulva and she responded by taking his engorged penis into her hand and stroking it gently. When he told her that the area immediately below the head was more sensitive than the head itself she encircled the shaft below the head with her thumb and fingers and caressed him, experimenting to find the combination of pressure of grip and movement which would give him the greatest pleasure. Their increasing intimacy led to his asking her if she would mind if he kissed the area between her legs, whereupon she immediately opened her thighs and, grasping his head, steered his tongue to the places where she felt the most pleasurable sensations. Her vulva became very moist. She asked if they could move so that she could kiss his penis while he continued to kiss her "down there." After they rearranged themselves she took the glans of his penis into her mouth and sucked it gently with evident pleasure before lapping the area immediately under the head with her tongue. He asked her if she felt ready for him to enter her and she said, "Darling, if you don't enter me soon I'm going to explode and I want to explode with you inside me!" So saying, she released his penis from her mouth, rolled on her back, kissed him and reached for the tube of jelly from the bedside cabinet. In a husky whisper she asked him to put some jelly on her. Very gently, he did so. Then she pulled him on top of her, exercising a degree of strength which surprised (and delighted) him, grasped his penis, guided it carefully into her vagina and brought her legs over his back so that she could draw him into her. As he started to move she urged him to thrust more strongly into her, whispering hoarsely, "Do me, darling, do me! You can thrust harder, darling, without hurting me and I want to feel that marvellous love maker of yours deep inside me where it now belongs. Until last night no one had made love to me and now I can't do without it! Oh, darling, I love you so much and I want you to do me again and again!" This time the virgin bride's climax was noisy in contrast to the earlier, almost silent one and her sheer animal enjoyment was evident to the delight of her new husband. The bedding of the virgin bride was an episode of lovemaking the role-playing David and Kate both found most satisfying.

By the time Kate became pregnant several months later, David's income had reached the level where it was possible for Kate to plan to give up work shortly before the baby was born and become a full-time mum after the birth.

During her pregnancy Kate began to keep a diary, as she wanted to record not only the events but also her feelings so that in the years to come she could, by reading the diary relive the momentous period in her life when she became a first time mother and remember how she adjusted to it. She enjoyed writing and as well as keeping the diary, she wrote an account of her life to date including her meeting David, their falling in love and their subsequent engagement and marriage. She kept the diary and notes in the old binder which still housed her record of the "Proceedings of the Institute of Advanced Sexology" – the discussions in the students' common room of the nurses' home which she had attended while a student. All were stowed away in the bottom of her wardrobe with copies of the nursing school gazette to which she had contributed and later edited.

Kate had become very close to David's mother, Anne, since

the engagement, so much so that Anne described Kate to her friends as the daughter she'd never had. Each felt genuine affection and respect for the other and by the time Kate became pregnant there was almost a mother and daughter relationship between Anne and her daughter-in-law, but one without the tensions often found between a woman and her biological daughter. During the pregnancy Kate, who was knowledgeable about pregnancy and birth because of her maternity department experience while training, was able to discuss any problems which concerned her with both her mother, an experienced nurse although by then she had not been nursing for over twenty years, and her mother-in-law, who was still practising as a doctor and continuing to perform surgery although she confined this to minor operations. So during her pregnancy, Kate had back up from a nurse and a doctor, both mothers themselves, and in addition from nursing friends, notably Judith, herself already a mother.

Very early in their relationship and later, Kate had remarked to David that if ever they had a son she would want him circumcised and on one occasion, half jokingly then, she had added that the circumcision should be postponed until after her six week post-partum check-up when she should be passed fit to "resume marital relations" and they would be able to celebrate her son's rite of passage appropriately. During her pregnancy, it was David who raised the question of circumcision if she gave birth to a boy, saying that he personally wanted any son of theirs circumcised and knew that she had always favoured circumcision, but that the NHS ban on circumcision meant that when their son went to school he was likely to be among a small minority of circumcised boys. Despite this he still favoured circumcision. He asked Kate how she felt about it. Kate said that she still considered it a sensible health measure, even if a boy's foreskin was fully retractable at birth, and her experience with David had confirmed her strong preference which extended to sons as well as husbands. She was sure that if a boy received a proper briefing from his parents before he started school and at intervals later, he would be able to give as good as he got if he was teased in the showers. "I haven't changed my mind at all," she said, "Don't forget I'm an acucullophiliac." It was nearly time to go to bed, so she added, "And a practising one, too!" and, seizing his hand, led him off for an early and mutually enjoyed bedtime.

Nevertheless, David's comment about a circumcised boy being in a minority concerned Kate enough to raise the issue with both prospective grandmothers. She broached the topic first with her own mother, asking her if she was to have another son, whether she would have him circumcised despite the decline in its incidence in Britain. Her mother countered by asking Kate if the real question shouldn't be whether a circumcision was going to be beneficial or detrimental to her grandson's long term health and that of any wife he married. She accepted that she was no longer active in nursing, but she knew of, and regretted, the NHS policy against elective circumcisions, which she thought a retrograde step in health care. She remained in favour of circumcision as a beneficial health measure and, therefore, a routine procedure where the choice was hers. She had discussed the fact that they had been circumcised with both her sons, Kate's brothers, while they were growing up and neither had shown any regrets but had registered approval – quite strong approval the last time it had been raised when they were in their teens. "If by some miracle, at my age I had another son I would certainly have him circumcised, NHS or no NHS, but it's you and David who have to decide what you both think is better for your child if it's a boy, dear."

Kate also sought advice from Anne. Bearing in mind the decline in the incidence of circumcision in Britain, did Anne have any advice for David and her in the event that they presented her with a grandson? Kate admitted that she had strongly held views of her own in favour of circumcision and told Anne how pleased she had been to find that David had been circumcised and that the operation had been so well performed. Anne beamed at her, and said that the first thing she wanted to say was how very relieved she was that Kate approved of her having had David circumcised – she had been worried that Kate, having gone through her nurse's training after the NHS had banned circumcision except where necessary for medical reasons, would have been exposed to the NHS propaganda disseminated in support of the ban and might have thought that she had not only exposed David to unnecessary and unwarranted surgery but caused him to be mutilated in a barbaric operation. From the time she realized that David and Kate were serious about each other and likely to become intimate, she had been apprehensive that Kate might well disapprove of the decision she had made over twenty years previously and Kate's approval had lifted a real weight off her mind.

Anne told Kate that after graduating from medical school, she had trained as a surgical assistant at the Royal Infirmary where she had performed many circumcisions before David's birth. Long before his birth, she had made up her mind that any son of hers, even one whose foreskin was short and fully retractable from the time he was born, would be circumcised because it promoted better health through greater hygiene - reducing the risk of cervical cancer in his future wife and for him eliminating any risk, however slight, of cancer of the penis. She also thought that it delayed orgasm in the male and therefore gave the female partner a better chance of attaining orgasm herself. "And it looks so much better," she added. Her husband, David's father, agreed with her views, but as the medically qualified parent, she bore the prime responsibility for the decision to circumcise David and when David took up with a nursing student, Anne had feared her future daughter-in-law's wrath would fall on her! She had had some concern about whom she should ask to circumcise David. Unlike some surgeons, she would never operate on her own child or any other close relative. She would need to find someone with the highest level of skill in performing circumcision and a lot of her colleagues admitted that the Jewish ritual circumcisions performed by mohelim were more skilfully performed than those by even very competent surgeons. She wasn't Jewish, but immediately after David's birth and some intense soul searching, she had contacted a mohel whose expertise had been praised by doctors and nurses alike and who took on non-religious cases. "Whenever I bathed David or changed his nappy I used to think that our mohel had done a lovely job. If I had had another baby boy I would have asked him to attend to him, too."

Anne added that the only time she had ever had any doubt about the wisdom of having had David circumcised was during 1940-41 when a German invasion of Britain seemed a real possibility and it had occurred to her that David's missing foreskin might be a passport to a German extermination camp for the whole family.

Anne commented that before the National Health Service was established, many doctors performed circumcisions on the basis of a parent's request. "I have always thought there was a strong case for all newborn baby boys to be circumcised. If a mother wanted her baby boy circumcised I did it. And if a mother asked my advice I would recommend circumcision even if the foreskin was short and retractable," she said. After the NHS made a policy decision to save money by refusing to perform the operation unless it was medically necessary, the number of circumcisions dropped quite dramatically, even though some doctors were more flexible than others in their views on what constituted medical necessity when faced with a parental request for a circumcision. The result was that circumcision had become relatively rare in Britain although routine infant circumcision before discharge was still the norm in the maternity departments of American and Canadian hospitals.

Anne asked Kate if she and David had reached any decision about circumcision if the baby was a boy. She thought it was important to decide before the baby was born so that they wouldn't feel pressured into making a rush decision during the short period between the birth and the discharge from hospital of mother and baby.

Kate said that she had wanted to talk to her mother and Anne before the birth in case either of them, as parents and medical professionals themselves, saw any serious problem in circumcising a boy knowing that the great majority of his contemporaries would not be circumcised. Or if, as parents, they had changed their minds about circumcision since having their own sons circumcised.

Anne said that when private patients asked for a baby boy to be circumcised, she still performed the operation on request whether it was medically necessary according to NHS criteria or not. "I still believe it should be a decision by the parents, not that of some NHS bureaucrat or accountant." Then she hesitated slightly before she said, "For what it's worth, if David was having a brother rather than a son, I would have him circumcised, even if that made him part of a minority among his schoolmates. I hope that makes my personal position clear, but, Kate dearest, it's you and David who will have to decide the fate of my grandson's foreskin, not me. What do you and David think?"

Kate said it had eased her mind to hear both Anne and her own mother come down firmly in favour of routine circumcision. Kate had already admitted to Anne her own strong bias in favour of circumcision and David was as happy with his own circumcised state as she was. Kate and he had discussed the question several times and had always concluded that that any son of theirs should be circumcised. They had addressed the issue of a circumcised boy being in a minority at school and decided that the benefit to health and sexual relations outweighed any such concern. The views of the prospective grandmothers coincided with their own.

One problem, and Kate thought it more acute now when fewer circumcisions were being done than when David and her brothers were born, was to find a competent circumciser for her baby. Before Anne had told her she didn't know that David had been circumcised by a mohel, nor, she thought, did David. She said to Anne that in fact she and David had already discussed having a medically qualified mohel circumcise the baby she was expecting if it was a boy. Her brother John, born in Alexandria, had been circumcised by a doctor who doubled as a mohel.

When Judith, her friend since they met at nursing school and who was Jewish, had a baby boy, she had asked Kate to attend the bris to assist the mohel and give moral support to

Judith. Kate told Anne she had been very impressed with the expertise of Judith's mohel who was a doctor in general practice and, thinking that one day she might have a baby herself, she had asked him after the ceremony if he took on non-religious cases. He told her that he did. He lived near their home. She knew that Judith had made careful inquiries about mohelim before choosing him to circumcise her baby. After the bris, Kate had suggested to David that if they ever had a son they might consider engaging his services. His name was Silverstein. "Oh yes," said Anne, "I know of him. Jewish friends of ours – the husband's a doctor - had him for their baby's bris and they were very satisfied indeed. I'm sure you won't find anyone better than him, Kate."

Anne reminded Kate that Prince Charles had been circumcised by the senior mohel of the Jewish community in London, Dr. Jacob Snowman, who was a general practitioner in Hampstead, and that by long standing tradition all British royal princes were circumcised by mohelim. She said "Funny, isn't it, Kate dear, that three non-Jewish medical professionals like your mother and you and me would desert our own profession in favour of a Jewish religious practitioner when we circumcise sons of our own?"

Kate and David's neighbours had given them a friendly welcome when they moved into their house. Sandra was one with whom Kate had struck up a close friendship and when Kate was at home, they often had coffee or tea together. Sandra and her husband Jeff were somewhat older than Kate and David but, like them, came from professional backgrounds. Sandra had two older sons from her first marriage and two children by her present husband, a three year old daughter and Stephen, who was born soon after Kate realized she was pregnant. The day after Sandra had come home from the maternity hospital with Stephen, Kate called to deliver a present for him and stayed for coffee with Sandra. Sandra said that the birth had gone well, but one thing had disturbed her and since Kate was a nurse, she would appreciate any advice Kate could give her. On the morning after Stephen's birth, thinking that she should arrange it well before she went home with him, she had asked for him to be circumcised before they were discharged from the hospital, only to be told that no babies were circumcised nowadays unless it was needed for medical reasons and it was not necessary in her son's case. Sandra said she was shocked and surprised. She had taken it up with the ward sister and the registrar but got the same negative response.

Her two sons of her first marriage had not been circumcised because their father was not circumcised and did not want them to be circumcised. The older boy hadn't had any problems but the younger one had a tight, unretractable foreskin and after recurrent infections he had been circumcised at the age of five, an experience sufficiently traumatic to make her wish that she had followed her mother's advice during her first pregnancy to have any baby son of hers circumcised as soon as possible after birth. Sandra told Kate that she had been a virgin when she married for the first time and had found the way her husband's prepuce retracted during erection very exciting but despite this she had never felt able to fellate him. Jeff, her present husband, had been "snipped," as she put it, as a baby and, although in a way she had regretted that the process of his erection was visually less dramatic, she liked the neat appearance of his penis and soon found, somewhat to her surprise, that she enjoyed taking his penis into her mouth. When she became pregnant by him, they had agreed that if she had a boy she should arrange for him to be circumcised. While pregnant she had actually tried to imagine what it would be like to bath her baby boy but that little boy of her imagination looked like his father and certainly hadn't had a foreskin to complicate bathing him.

Now the hospital had sent her home with a son who, contrary to his parents' wishes, had not been circumcised and whose prepuce could not be retracted. Surely parents had some rights in matters like this? Kate told Sandra she agreed completely with her that circumcision should be available on the parents' request. Sandra asked her if the baby she was carrying turned out to be a son, would she want him circumcised, and Kate told her that she would, and that she would be going outside the NHS to have him circumcised. She asked Sandra if she had considered having the operation done privately.

After Sandra asked if Kate could help her in getting Stephen circumcised as a private patient, Kate mentioned that her own mother-in-law, Anne, was a surgeon experienced in the operation and that Kate had assisted her in several infant circumcisions and could vouch for her skill and competence. Anne often did circumcisions at the parents' own home and if Sandra wanted Anne to circumcise Stephen, she could bring Anne to Sandra's house and, as an experienced theatre nurse, assist Anne at the circumcision and come in on the days following the operation to change the dressings. Sandra thanked Kate for her suggestion and said she would talk it over with Jeff and phone Kate. That evening Sandra phoned Kate to tell her that she and Jeff would like Anne to undertake the surgery and that they were anxious to get it done as soon as possible while Stephen was a matter of days rather than weeks old.

The day before Stephen's circumcision Kate went round to Sandra's house to make arrangements for the operation scheduled for the following morning. Kate gave Sandra the time at which Stephen should receive a final feeding before the operation so that his stomach would be empty at the time set for his circumcision to avoid his vomiting during surgery. Sandra said she felt she should be present at the circumcision to support her son and breastfeed him immediately afterwards to comfort him and because he would be hungry. Kate had been at circumcisions where the mothers had insisted on being with their babies and knew that most mothers found it a trying experience, so she persuaded Sandra to leave her and Anne with Stephen and go over to Kate's nearby house and make herself a cup of coffee or tea. Kate promised to phone her as soon as the operation had been completed so that she could come back and give Stephen his feed just as quickly as if she had stayed with him. Kate explained to Sandra that young babies like Stephen were circumcised without an anaesthetic because it was a very quick operation and there were risks in giving an anaesthetic to a very young child. At a Jewish circumcision, the baby usually sucked on a sugar cube wrapped in gauze which had been soaked in wine or brandy and she thought this gave the baby considerable relief. Unless Sandra had any objection to Stephen being given alcohol, Kate would borrow David's bottle of brandy and bring it, sugar cubes and gauze and let Stephen suck on this simple analgesic for a while before the operation began and during it. Sandra agreed and thanked Kate for thinking of it, saying she knew her baby would be in good hands.

The next morning while Kate was prepping Stephen for his circumcision, Anne remarked that being a woman she always had in mind that the small patient she was circumcising would be some girl's husband one day and this spurred her to aim for a good cosmetic result as well as surgical accuracy. Her patient's future bride was entitled to a husband with a penis whose function and appearance had not been marred by the removal of too much skin or the presence of an untidy excess of skin or skin tags or skin bridges due to faulty technique on her part. When he wasn't erect, his bride was entitled to a husband with a completely exposed glans and a neat, regular and nearly invisible scar line. Anne laughed as she told Kate that although she had performed lots of circumcisions before she married she had only formulated what she called the bride's bill of rights after she herself became a bride. Her own subsequent motherhood had given new emphasis to her views on the importance of surgical accuracy and cosmetic appearance. As Anne deftly removed Stephen's foreskin, she commented to Kate that Stephen's glans was well shaped but the glans penis came in a variety of shapes - some attractive and some less so - and one couldn't do anything about that, but one could, and should, always be careful to perform a neat circumcision.

While Anne was expounding her bride's bill of rights, Kate was thinking of the first time she had seen Anne's own son's penis during their inaugural bath together. She blushed at the recollection. Technically, but only technically she reminded herself, she hadn't been a bride at the time, but having heard Anne's views on the importance of the bride's reaction she felt that Anne might like to be reassured about Anne's own decision to circumcise her son and the end result – she smiled inwardly as she appreciated her unspoken and unintended pun. "You know already how delighted this bride is that her mother-in-law had her bridegroom circumcised, but I want you to know that when I first saw David nude I thought what a beautiful penis he had – a shapely head and just the right amount of skin removed to give him a completely bare glans and no surplus skin on the shaft, whether erect or flaccid. I was grateful to you then, but it's only now while we are working together on someone else's baby's circumcision and I have heard your bride's bill of rights that I feel liberated enough to tell you not only how happy I am that you had David circumcised, but that you found someone to do it who had the combination of skill and care which gave him the same perfect surgical and cosmetic result that you have just given Stephen." Anne's eyes sparkled above her surgical mask and, pointing at it, she told Kate, "If I hadn't got this thing on, I'd kiss you for saying that here and now, so remind me later I owe you a big one and a heartfelt hug!"

Later when Kate came over to Sandra's to check Stephen's dressing for signs of bleeding, Sandra expressed her relief at how well he had come through his circumcision, which she realized must have been painful. She smiled as she said she had been able to smell brandy on Stephen's breath as she fed him and commented that he had slept well afterwards. Kate told her about an occasion when she was a student nurse in the maternity department and one of her patients, who was Jewish, had not been well enough to attend her baby's bris which had been held at the hospital, so Kate had taken the baby to the ceremony and brought him back to his mother to be fed. Later, when she went to collect the baby after his feed, the mother told her that she knew a baby was given wine at his bris but hers had imbibed so well that he was drunk. "Mind you," she said, "I'm glad. If I was having that done to me, I'd rather be drunk, blind drunk!"

Kate checked Stephen's dressing twice more that day and after her last visit she walked the short distance back home to await David's return from a dinner with a client. Anne's remarks about the bride's bill of rights had excited her and she could not get them out of her mind – not that she tried very hard. This contributed to her feeling sensuous and, as she had had her supper and David would have eaten, she did not have to prepare a meal and she thought an early night together would be a pleasant way of ending their day. Soon after returning home, she heard David's car in the driveway and went outside to greet him with an invitation to have a bath with her. David always enjoyed a shared bath and they were soon soaping and rinsing each other in their usual sensuous way. As he knelt opposite her to be washed by her, she asked him if he had ever heard of the bride's bill of rights. He hadn't, so she recited it, adding that it was very important to her. She asked if he could guess who the author was. He said it must be a woman, but couldn't hazard a guess beyond "some consumers' group – good for them!" She told him it was his own mother and went on to say how much she admired her professionally as a surgeon and loved her as a person. Kate said that she was lucky to have such a mother-in-law, but that as a bride she was also lucky that her mother-in-law had ensured that her bridegroom complied in full measure with the bill of rights. Then she leaned forward to kiss the subject of the bill which further excited it. They went into the bedroom together and as they tumbled into bed she explained that she had been waiting for most of that day for him to return and make love to her and needed the sexual release he was going to give her. They were both ready for each other; Kate's pent up desire meant that that she was well lubricated and the attention she had given him in the bath ensured that he slid into her easily as they satisfied each other's needs before falling into a sound slumber in each other's arms.

A few days after the circumcision, when Kate was removing Stephen's final dressing and the wound was well on the way to healing, she showed Sandra the result of Anne's neat surgery. Sandra was very pleased and said, "I know it sounds awful, but I have become used to the tidy appearance of a circumcised penis and I did not like the appearance of my little fellow's prepuce. I was not looking forward to bathing him as he got older and having to pull back a foreskin, which I didn't think he should still have when he left hospital, to wash under it. Now, thanks to your mother-in-law and you, and absolutely no thanks to the National Health Service, I have a baby whose essential equipment looks right and I'm grateful to both of you."

When her nursing school friend and mentor, Margaret, had a baby Kate noted in her diary on successive days –

"Margaret booked in today to have her baby by caesarean because of her placenta previa and I went to see her in the private room she has mysteriously managed to wangle. She's promised to let me know how she fixed it so I can get one when my time comes. She's excited and looking forward to having her baby. She told me that on arriving in her room she found a patient report form had been posted at the end of her bed. She had read it, of course. "It looked wholly authentic. Obviously prepared and left by you or another of my alleged friends. It described me as "an elderly primipara." Thanks a bundle - I'm only 27! When I find out the guilty party I'm going to exact a terrible revenge before I leave." Luckily she was laughing – she's done worse in her time. I did not admit guilt."

"Margaret had her caesarean this morning and has a healthy boy, 7lb 4oz. She was back in her private room by the time I could get away to see her. She was still woozy from the anaesthetic, but excited about the baby. I saw him and he's fine. Good looking as caesarean babies usually are."

"Margaret phoned and asked me to drop in when I came off duty. When I visited her she said she had arranged for Mr. Wilson to circumcise her son tomorrow. Asked if I would assist him. She has assisted him at several circumcisions and has a high regard for his ability and care. Having assisted myself at some of his circumcisions, so do I. M is a great fixer and says she can arrange for my "temporary attachment" to W who is coming in specially to do the circumcision as a favour to M. M says she will attend. I tried to dissuade her, but she feels she is responsible for what is being done to her baby and insists on being there to support him through it."

"Today I assisted Mr Wilson FRCS at Margaret's baby's circumcision. M phoned me early this morning and said she'd developed an infection and wouldn't be allowed out of bed to attend the circumcision as she had planned. I went round to see her in her room well ahead of the slated time to find out how she was and to try to cheer her up as she sounded a mite tearful on the phone. En route to M's room I checked with the sister and was told the infection was not serious but she was on antibiotics, so not allowed to continue breastfeeding and feeling a bit low. I was glad I had gone earlier than was scheduled to pick up the baby and take him along to the treatment room for his op – it gave me the chance to sit with M for a few minutes and chat, which she obviously welcomed, and I hope helped her. She told me that she had asked Wilson to make sure he took off enough skin to make her son "a real roundhead" like her husband. I asked her if she had discussed having the baby's frenulum removed and she said it hadn't been mentioned but she would like it done and would I ask Wilson? She said that although she had always been determined to have any son of hers circumcised because of the benefits of the operation, when it actually came to handing her baby over for it to be performed, she lost her objectivity as a nurse and became anxious about the pain he would suffer - like any other mother, but worse for her because she had assisted at circumcisions herself. She said she was trying to comfort herself with the thought "short term pain for long term gain", but at this moment all she could think about was the pain. She asked me to hold the baby myself during the op and comfort him for her as well as I could. When the time came for me to pick up the baby she cuddled him for a while and talked to him saying that what was going to be done to him would hurt a lot but it would be better for him when he grew up and had a wife to make love to because she would appreciate his circumcision "just as Mummy appreciates Daddy's." As she handed him to me she began to cry. I did my best to reassure her and promised to bring him back safe and sound as soon as it was all over, but she was still tearful when I left the room. As I went by the sister's desk I told her and asked her to drop by M's room to make sure she was alright.

"I took the baby down to the treatment room where one of

the maternity wing nurses helped me prep the baby before Mr. Wilson's arrival. When he came I passed on to him M's wish that the frenulum be removed. W nodded assent.

"I sat on a chair holding the baby on my lap and W sat opposite me with the instrument tray by him and the maternity nurse passing the instruments. Unlike many newborn boys Margaret's baby had a foreskin which could be drawn back easily, as M had told me and I had confirmed while prepping him, and had reported to W, so W was able to retract it and save the baby from the pain caused by using a probe to break down adhesions preliminary to excising the foreskin. W was able to expose the head of the penis fully before pulling the skin forward again and applying forceps in front of the glans, setting them at an angle parallel to the corona of the glans. He then cut away the foreskin using the forceps as a guide for his scalpel, and trimmed away the inner layer of the foreskin which was still covering most of the glans, so that the head of the baby's penis was fully exposed, remarking to me as he did that "Margaret is going to take home the genuine roundhead she wants," and then excised the frenulum. W put in stitches to proximate the cut edges and applied Vaseline and a dressing. The baby had begun to cry at the beginning of the op when the forceps were applied and had screamed while his foreskin and frenulum were being excised and during the stitching. I had tried to comfort him by talking to him as I held him tightly to keep him immobile for the surgery, but by now the poor little thing was worn out by his screaming and crying and I was glad that M hadn't been there to hear him - newborn circumcisions are not for the faint-hearted since anaesthesia is not used for safety reasons. After W left to visit M and tell her that everything had gone well, I stayed in the treatment room with the baby in my arms and cuddled him to try to make up for the ordeal he had been through until he was settled before taking him back to M's room.

"On the way I picked up at the nursing station the bottle feed which I had ordered earlier to be made ready after the op was over. By the time I got to M's room W had left and M took the baby from my arms and gave him the bottle feed which had

had to be delayed until the op was over so that he wouldn't vomit and perhaps choke under the stress of the surgery. I had wanted to give it to him in the treatment room before bringing him back to M as I knew he was hungry and the feed would comfort him, but it seemed better to let M give it to him so that she would see that he was alright and have the pleasure of caring for him. M was relieved it was all over. W had repeated the "genuine roundhead" quip to her. She asked if I had been satisfied with the op and I told her that I thought she was going to be very pleased with the result when the bandage came off and she was able to see her baby's modified penis for herself. I told her that if he was my baby I would be very happy and that I was sure that the circumcision was a very neat one, the glans was going to be completely bare, the line of the circumcision should be invisible or nearly so after healing and the frenulum neatly excised. I checked him later several times for signs of bleeding and there were none. I made the last check and saw M just before I went home and, with the baby's op over, she seemed more settled."

"The day after Margaret's baby's circumcision. I changed his dressing in the treatment room and then saw M and told her that the wound was healing nicely. She's still rather low due to the infection but the antibiotic seems to be clearing it. Baby doing well."

"The second day after Margaret's baby's circumcision. M was feeding him in her room and I waited until she had finished before changing his dressing. M's infection has responded well to the antibiotic and she's feeling much better so I took her to the treatment room with me so that she could see for herself her baby's penis in its new circumcised form when I took the dressing off. She was very pleased and, being M, said "Don't laugh at me, please, Kate, but I do feel that by having my baby son circumcised, so that the glans of his penis has been made completely and permanently bare, I am preparing him to be a husband and father. Both the men in my life now have proper penises, both full-blown roundheads. What more could a girl want?" She asked me if I still planned to have my baby circumcised if a boy and I told her that, although I had never made love with anyone other than David, my experiences with him had reinforced my conviction that all males should be circumcised. Then I said "You know, I do agree with you that when we women, or some of us, anyway, arrange for our sons to be circumcised we are, consciously or unconsciously, preparing them for lovemaking. Even when it isn't erect a circumcised penis with a bare glans looks ready for making love in a way that an uncircumcised penis does not. Even if a mother requests a circumcision for her son and cites a reason, say, improved hygiene, I'm sure that many of them, consciously or not, have this subliminal urge to reshape a son's penis so that it looks ready to fulfil its sexual role. I admit it's one of the several reasons why I am determined that any son of mine will have a cirk. I hope his will look as good as your baby's. You've done the right thing in having your son circumcised and I am sure that neither you nor he nor your daughter-in-law will ever regret it." I didn't add that if her son had been asked mid-op two days ago he would certainly have expressed a different opinion.

"Before I left her M said that the sight of her husband Ian's circumcised penis was always a real turn-on for her, whether it was erect or "at rest". One night two or three weeks before the baby was due, in bed and unable to sleep, "out of devilment" she had switched on the bedside light and turned to Ian who as usual was sleeping very soundly and tried to find out if she could make him erect and ejaculate without waking him up. "All in the interests of science," she claimed. "Don't forget good old lust, too," I prompted. She had pulled the bed clothes down stealthily to reveal Ian's flaccid penis with its bare head fully exposed to her view and grasped his penis, tracing the scar line of his circumcision just below the head of his relaxed penis with her forefinger thinking as she did so that if she had a son she would want him to have a nice neat circumcision just like his father's. As she did this Ian's penis became magnificently erect at her touch and she continued to play with it gently until he awoke to find her with his glans in her mouth. She explained to him she couldn't sleep and she had been thinking about the circumcision they had agreed their baby would have if a boy. She told me that she felt really randy and at that moment desperately wanted Ian to "fuck" her but, of course, she realized she was much too far gone in her pregnancy for that and they had had to settle for his fondling her breasts and her bringing him to climax by a combination of hand and mouth. But she said it had been a wonderful, memorable experience as they were both very turned on by the thought of their baby being circumcised to make him look like his father and she had brought Ian to a really explosive climax while his penis was in her mouth. She wondered how many couples had circumcision fantasies like that one or acted out circumcisions with the woman pretending to circumcise her man. "It made me realize how important a part circumcision plays in my sex life and how much I appreciate having a circumcised husband and lover," she said. I responded by asking her - in a suitably supercilious way! – if she realized that she was a certifiable acucullophiliac. "What on earth's that?" she asked suspiciously. I told her airily that it was an advanced and incurable form of nymphomania where the nymphomaniac could only be satisfied by a circumcised penis. "Oh, my God!" she said, "Surely I'm not that bad?" I couldn't keep my face straight any longer, and told her how I'd found the item about acucullophilia and its (proper) definition in the magazine someone had left in a hotel lounge. "Oh, that's alright," she said, looking quite relieved, "you gave me a nasty fright then, for a moment, but if I've got it so have you. And, unlike someone I know, I never had to go and ask advice about how to find out if my boyfriend was qualified to screw a raging acucullophiliac!" She laughed so hard and for so long that I feared for her sutures! But I went away satisfied that she was well on the road to recovery.

"David works hard and values his beauty sleep but M has planted a seed in my mind for the next time I wake up in the middle of the night with my helpmeet slumbering peacefully next to me. D has never complained about being wakened up by a sexual assault in the past and I expect he'll find a reprise of M's evening entertainment as much an aphrodisiac as I know I will. Thanks, Margaret, for the idea.

"I'm glad Margaret said she wanted him to "fuck" her. It's a word I don't usually feel I should use but in the context M used it has to be the RIGHT word. "Make love" or "have intercourse" are just too anodyne to express how she felt. What she wanted then was for him to "fuck" her – she obviously wanted something more than genteel lovemaking – and she might have gone further and said something like "I want your big stiff cock inside me and I need you to fuck me." Words like "fuck" and "cock" are okay in that context, I think, probably because neither word is used in a derogatory or demeaning sense – actually, in quite the opposite sense. But, logically or illogically, I don't feel the same way about "prick," "cunt" or "twat" which I think are always derogatory and demeaning and don't like and won't use.

"I'm even gladder that Margaret and her husband found circumcision a sexual turn-on – just as D and I do. I have often thought – and worried – that I was unusual in being so interested in circumcision and making it something of a fetish of mine. Since I read that magazine item about acucullophilia I have known that I'm not alone, but I'm glad that someone as rational and well-balanced as M is similarly inclined. My interest in circumcision began before I reached my teens, in Alexandria when Joan's baby had to be circumcised and Mum had my little brother Roger circumcised. I used to be bathed with my brother John and I took his acorn tipped penis for granted, not realising that there were two optional styles of penis available. By the time I entered nursing school the NHS had effectively banned circumcision but I got used to seeing males of both types and came to realize that sexually I much preferred the appearance of the circumcised variety. I have never had a sexual encounter with anyone but David and consequently cannot make a comparison based on personal experience in terms of sexual performance, but he certainly satisfies me sexually. I am convinced that circumcision is beneficial on health and sexual grounds to the man and his sexual partner, and aesthetically preferable as well."

David and Kate had always slept together in the nude which

they found had very practical advantages, particularly in initiating lovemaking. They often fell asleep facing each other in each other's arms, he cupping a breast or touching her vulva and she holding his penis. In the early stages, her pregnancy made little difference to their sleeping habits and their sexual desire for each other remained as strong throughout, but eventually her burgeoning belly led to Kate finding that the most comfortable way to lie in bed was on her side and thereafter they often made love facing each other lying on their sides. They found they could still enjoy 69 sessions. Now when they went to sleep they often slept on their sides with Kate's slender and shapely bottom towards David and he facing her back with an arm around her and often with his penis in mutually pleasurable contact with her bottom. One advantage of Kate's pregnancy was that they didn't have any need for contraception. As time went by Kate found that she was waking more often during the night, sometimes because she had been sleeping in a position which became uncomfortable and as she reached the third trimester because the baby was pressing on her bladder and she needed to make nocturnal visits to the bathroom. When she woke she often felt sexual desire and if she could not get back to sleep she did not hesitate to rouse David and tell him of her need for him. As they usually went to bed early enough to spend a long night together and as David loved Kate and welcomed any sexual initiative on her part, her sleeplessness gave rise to many episodes of lovemaking which both later looked back on with great pleasure.

One night Kate had woken and lain awake, turning over in her mind the childbirth plan she had been putting into written form during the day before David came home. She got towards the end of the plan and was rehearsing the arrangements she had planned for a circumcision in the event she had a son. Frequently during her pregnancy, she had found herself wondering whether she was going to give birth to a boy or a girl – it could be either and she had to plan for either contingency so her birth plan had to allow for a child of either gender. She knew she wanted any son of hers to be circumcised and she was satisfied about the practical health and hygienic advantages of the operation and the aesthetic considerations which were also important to her, but as an expectant mother she dreaded the pain that her nursing experience made her aware was inevitable for her baby. So, in addition to the health, hygienic and aesthetic benefits which she fully acknowledged, she thought of her son's circumcision in terms of pain as well as pleasure – the pain he would suffer during an admittedly short operation as well as the increased sexual pleasure which she hoped he and any girl he married would enjoy as a result of his being circumcised. During the operation she would be there to share his pain and support him, but afterwards every time she bathed him, she would feel pleasure in the knowledge that she was the mother of a circumcised son – a thought she instantly recognized as honest but, in terms of it being her personal preference, selfish. "Short term pain for long term gain" – that summed it up; it was what Margaret had said to her about her own baby's circumcision and she was right. Her worries receded and she thought of the bride's bill of rights enunciated by her mother-in-law, beginning a mental progression which led to much happier thoughts.

Then she remembered Margaret's hilarious account of her assault on her sleeping Ian late in her pregnancy and, much cheered, decided to try a similar experiment on David. She switched the bedside light on and drew the sheet and blankets down to reveal her naked husband still sleeping soundly. His penis was relaxed when she took it in her hand, but at her touch slowly became erect. Like Margaret, she gently traced the line of his circumcision just below and around the base of his bare glans using the nail of her forefinger. As she did this she was imagining how her own son, if it was a boy she was carrying within her, would be circumcised. She found it a very sensuous thought. Even though it would be very painful for him and a traumatic experience for her, she knew that she would never be happy if a son of hers, even one born with a fully retractable foreskin, did not have a circumcision. As she looked at the exposed head of her slumbering husband's penis she realized yet again that for her, a circumcision was an imperative for any husband or son of hers. There were hygienic and health considerations as well as aesthetic advantages, but as she looked at David's penis and ran her fingernail lightly around it again she acknowledged to herself that the very fact itself that he had been circumcised gave her great sexual pleasure and she admitted to herself that in some sexual way, less overtly sexual than her lustful feelings about David's circumcision, it was important to her happiness that that her son should undergo a circumcision, a full circumcision, so that his penis too would have a permanently exposed head.

She was conscious now of the same need that Margaret had felt in similar circumstances for her husband to make love to her but, fortunately for her, unlike Margaret, she was not so far advanced in her pregnancy that full penetrative intercourse was not possible. Yet another time, she ran her fingernail around his penis, still thinking about David's circumcision and the possibility that she would soon be present at the circumcision of her own son. This time she must have pressed her nail more firmly into David's flesh because he woke to find the light on, the bedclothes pulled down and this sensuous wife of his running her fingernail around the most sensitive part of his penis, unmistakably pretending to circumcise him. He already knew, of course, how much Kate cherished the fact that he had been circumcised and now she told him that as she had been touching him she had been imagining the circumcision of their son if the baby she was carrying was a boy and said she felt sure she was going to give birth to a son. If it was a boy, they had already agreed that he would be circumcised and her imagining so graphically their baby's circumcision had given her such strong sexual longings that she urgently needed him to make love to her as attaining orgasm was the only way she could go back to sleep after becoming so sexually aroused.

Then she went on, "Darling, I do want our baby to be a boy and I want him to be circumcised because of all the advantages it will give him, but I also know that it's going to hurt him like hell while it's being done. To strengthen me in my resolve to have him circumcised I want you, his father and my husband and lover, to make love to me with your circumcised penis now so that I can experience it deep within me and be reassured by the love you give me with a penis which has been circumcised just as our son's penis will be circumcised." Her words further excited him and she felt his penis became even stiffer and the bulbous head throbbed in her hand. Her pregnancy was too far advanced for him to lie above her as they made love. She leaned over him to kiss him and he lifted his arms to help her climb above him as he lay on his back. Having straddled him, she again grasped his penis, pulled downwards on the skin of his shaft and guided his very erect and aroused penis into her vagina which was very wet indeed due to the intensity of her arousal. Then she began to move up and down on him rhythmically and whispered huskily again and again that she could feel his lovely, circumcised cock deep inside her, exciting her and helping her find the relief she needed so much. She began to moan, first softly and then more loudly as she neared her orgasm. They both came, she very noisily. She remained astraddle him for a while with his now limp penis inside her until, with his help, she moved to lie beside him facing towards him. She took his penis in her hand, encircling it with her forefinger and thumb just below the head and said in a low husky voice which was full of emotion, "Thank you, darling, for the sexual relief you have given me and even more for the wonderful reassurance I now feel. It's not always going to be easy to be a conscientious mum, but after you give me an orgasm like that one I feel ready for anything, so I'm going to ask you to make love to me to strengthen me immediately before any son of ours is circumcised and again after our son's ordeal is over to comfort me by making love to me again. Not just once but several times before and several times afterwards – I shall need you and I shall need it, darling! Just seeing your circumcised penis makes me happy, but having it perform like it just did confirms me in my resolve that any son of ours must be circumcised, not only for his own benefit but also to ensure that he will be able to do for his wife what you have just done for me. That's the true intent underlying your mother's bill of rights for brides and, thanks to her; I've got all the rights a bride could ever want."

Chapter 11

Genesis

Kate came home with her son James, who had been immediately nicknamed Jimmy, a week after his birth and two days later, Kate's diary recorded a visit from her friend Sandra –
"Sandra came to visit today to see Jimmy for the first time, bringing with her a lovely little matinee jacket for Jimmy from her and Jeff. I was changing Jimmy on the very swish fold-up changing table and baby bath which Anne gave us when the doorbell rang and I strapped Jimmy down on the table while I went to bring Sandra and Stephen in, so her first sight of our son and heir was of him in the altogether. She said what a nice-looking baby he is – I must admit I think so, too – and then she said "So you haven't had him circumcised yet." Knowing how I feel about circumcision I could see she was obviously surprised. "No, we're going to wait until after I've had my post-partum check-up six weeks after the birth." "Is there some advantage in delaying it?" asked Sandra. Sandra and I are close enough friends to share confidences and I told her the true reason, saying "The delay isn't going to make it any more painful or a worse ordeal for Jimmy. The delay will be for me. The truth is that until I've had my six-week check-up and passed it David and I can't make love. David was circumcised as a baby and his circumcision has always been very precious to me. Before Jimmy has his little op and after it's all over I shall want David to make love to me - beforehand to strengthen me for it and afterwards to give me the comforting I know I shall need and to celebrate the new bond the circumcision will create between the

three of us. I hope you won't think I'm odd or selfish about this, but I do feel a strong need for it." "No," said Sandra thoughtfully. "No. I certainly don't think there's anything odd or strange about it. In fact I think it's a really lovely idea. I just wish I'd had the same thought before we asked Dr. Anne to circumcise our little one when he was two and a half weeks old. Damn, we shouldn't have been in such a hurry. We've obviously missed out. Jeff and I have always thought of circumcision as a very erotic topic. My first husband wasn't circumcised and one of the many joys of my honeymoon with Jeff was getting acquainted with his circumcised penis. I married Jeff before my second son had his circumcision and I had never seen a circumcised penis before, let alone an adult one, so it was all new to me. One day while we were on honeymoon, we were in the bath together before going to bed and I was feeling particularly sensuous. I was washing his penis and exploring it when a sudden thought came to me and I said to him "Darling, when we have a baby boy of our own I shall want him to be circumcised so that he will be a roundhead just like you!" The thought had excited me, and it excited Jeff as well. He was already erect, but as my words sank in he became rock hard and he lifted me out of the bath and carried me to bed where we had a particularly lustful session, even by our honeymoon standards! Yes, yours is a super idea. If I have another son we'll be asking Dr. Anne to wield her scalpel again, but next time it will be after, not before, I've had my check-up."

Three weeks after Jimmy was born, Kate's diary read –

"Jimmy has been sleeping right through the night for a while now and I feel much less tired than I did when I first got back home with him. David was able to take a day off work today, so I thought it would be nice to invite the new grandparents and Judith and her little Michael round for lunch. As befitted the occasion I dressed Jimmy in the smartest outfit he had been given. Just before the guests arrived - and having dressed him in his very best clothes I should have expected it, I suppose – Jimmy had an almighty "accident," one of such magnitude that it required an immediate bath and a complete change of outfit. He was still in the baby bath in the living room when our guests arrived and joined in the fun while David served drinks and pre-lunch refreshments. Trust Mum! She took one look at Jimmy's little plonker and asked whether it was going to be "attended to," as she delicately put it, soon. I should have been ready for it, I suppose, but bearing in mind the real reason for the delay, I hesitated before replying while I thought out a plausible excuse. That perceptive girl Judith, who knows very well the reason for the delay, and realized instinctively that I needed some time for thought before replying to Mum, jumped in to give me the respite I desperately needed, by remarking how lucky I was that I hadn't had to go through her experience of leaving hospital to make arrangements for a bris and big reception on the eighth day after giving birth while she was still exhausted. Finally I told Mum – with that wicked girl Judith grinning evilly at me – that David and I had thought it best to delay Jimmy's circumcision until his feeding patterns were well established. Anne, quite innocently, backed me. I don't want Mum nagging me about Jimmy's circumcision so the sooner I can tell her it's been arranged the better! Memo: call Judith's mohel Dr. Silverstein tomorrow to check his availability 4 weeks from now and make sure of a date when D can be at home, Judith available to act as nurse and Anne and Mum able to attend if they wish – neither grandpa will want to come, I'm sure: men find these things too traumatic – too near to home, I guess! Also contact my obstetrician to book my 6 week check-up no later than 3 weeks from today – I must get my "licence" back with time to spare before Dr. S's attendance on Jimmy."

Six weeks to the day after Jimmy's birth Kate recorded in her diary that her obstetrician had signed her off after she passed her six week post-partum check up. "Yippee, got my sex licence back. Memo: call Dr. Silverstein tomorrow am to make a provisional appointment re Jimmy here at our house and then call David, Judith, Mum and Anne before going firm on date and time." The diary doesn't record what happened after David got back home from the office that evening but Jimmy was put down to sleep earlier than usual and dinner was very late coming to table.

A week later Kate wrote-

"C Day minus 1. When I bathed Jimmy this morning I tried gently once again to retract his foreskin (which is quite long and tight) but I could only expose the very tip of his little glans so tomorrow Dr. Silverstein will have to start from scratch and loosen the adhesions before he can do the actual operation. This is unfortunate; I had hoped to be able to retract his prepuce behind the glans and spare him the additional pain of having the adhesions separated and the extra time he has to be restrained. Judith came over pm to discuss the arrangements for tomorrow and also attempted retraction but did no better than me. She says that Michael was just the same, and we agreed that most very young boys we had looked after had unretractable foreskins. I phoned Mum and asked her if I could borrow her old armless kitchen chair so that Judith can sit on it with Jimmy on her lap tomorrow. "Of course," she said, "and you might as well keep it." I laughed to myself trying to imagine what Mum would say if she knew that chair's secret history. She must realize that I got deflowered somewhere but she doesn't know when or where and I'm sure she would have a fit if she knew her old kitchen chair was the venue of that particular event in our family history. It seems appropriate that having used it to lose my maidenhood, it should play a part when my first born loses his foreskin. Drove to Mum and Dad's with Jimmy to pick up the chair."

The next day Kate's diary entry was much longer than usual –

"C Day. David took this morning off work and, bless him, left me asleep while he got up to make me a cup of tea and brought it to me, so we enjoyed the luxury of tea together in bed while Jimmy was still peacefully asleep. D cuddled me and held me which helped to calm the apprehension which, like any mother, I felt about the day ahead of us – I found that being a nurse (and an acucullophiliac to boot) didn't save me from being very jittery. When D kissed me I reached downwards to find that the prototype for today's proceedings was very much alive and well! One advantage of sleeping au naturel as we do is that time spent in removing pyjamas and nightie is saved. We kissed and cuddled for a while before I guided D's rampant organ into me and he made much needed love to me very gently. It improved my morale no end to reflect that the penis which was giving me such pleasure had itself undergone the procedure that my son was about to undergo. Afterwards Jimmy was still asleep and D and I slipped quietly into the bathroom to share a bath. Looking at D's penis I thought how truly elegant it looked with its bare, ready to go head and the shaft covered with smooth unwrinkled skin with none to spare and knew we have made the right decision for our young James as Anne had done for D long ago, and I felt good about it.

"When Jimmy woke we bathed him and I showed D that his foreskin wouldn't go back. I couldn't feed him before the op because of the risk of his vomiting and choking on the vomit, so I had arranged with Dr. Silverstein as early an appointment as possible, but the poor little thing was already hungry and fretful. Judith arrived first and changed into surgical kit so that she would be ready to assist Dr. S and help me with Jimmy. Following an old Jewish tradition, Judith took some lumps of sugar, wrapped them in small pieces of cotton gauze and dipped them in D's best brandy to serve as an analgesic and we put one between Jimmy's lips for him to suck on as a sedative. He gave every sign of enjoying it. Mum and Anne arrived together – it's great that they are such good friends. Finally Dr. S arrived, bang on schedule, gave Judith and me our instructions, put up a folding table that he had brought with him for the instruments and inspected and approved the chairs that he and Judith were to sit on. I watched him setting out his instruments. Thank God I'm a nurse – I didn't feel queasy. Not much, anyway. I noticed D didn't look at all good and hoped that at the critical moment he wouldn't seize his own plonker, faint and fall on the floor as Judith with her experience of brisses had – rather too cheerfully, I thought – predicted might enliven the proceedings.

"I told Dr. S that I had tried to retract Jimmy's foreskin but failed and he said it was not unusual not to be able to pull back such a young baby's prepuce. I reminded him that we wanted him to remove Jimmy's frenulum and told him that the mohel who had circumcised David had not left any more skin than was needed for erection and the line of the incision was immediately below his glans. "Please give Jimmy the same kind of circumcision," I asked, "I want them to be a matching pair." Dr. S smiled and said he would be glad to oblige as that was how he himself thought a circumcision should be performed.

"All was now ready. Realizing this, Mum picked up Jimmy, kissed and cuddled him and handed him to Anne who did likewise before giving him to a palpably nervous David. D hugged and kissed him before passing him to Judith, who beckoned me over and very quietly asked me if I wanted to go outside into the garden and take David with me. "No," I said, "remember I'm a nurse and I WANT my baby circumcised. I'm not going to run away from it, Judith. Nor David. We're here to support our baby." Judith sat down on the old kitchen chair with Jimmy on her lap. I bent down, unpinned Jimmy's nappy and took it off, had one last look at his little hooded penis, picked him up, hugged and kissed him, returned him to Judith, nodded to Dr. S and moved away.

"Judith placed another brandy-soused sugar lump between Jimmy's lips and he sucked on it with evident enjoyment. Dr. S, sitting opposite her, edged his chair closer and, as instructed by him, she grasped Jimmy's little legs very firmly so that he couldn't move. Dr. S applied an antiseptic liberally to Jimmy's penis and then tried, like Judith and me before him, to retract Jimmy's foreskin. Jimmy began to cry. Dr. S couldn't move it any further than we had done and picked up a probe which he inserted carefully in the opening of the foreskin and pushed it gently downwards between the glans and the prepuce. By now Jimmy was deeply distressed, his face a deep red and he was crying and screaming. As Dr. S worked the probe to break down the adhesions between the glans and the foreskin he continued to scream - no wonder, poor kid, it must have been excruciatingly painful in spite of the brandy. When Dr. S had worked the probe right around the glans he was able to pull the foreskin back to reveal a very red little glans and some bleeding caused by the tearing of the adhesions. Although I have seen quite a few circumcisions, this was my baby and I hoped it would soon be over so that I could comfort him and give him his delayed breakfast – the poor mite was not only in pain, he was hungry too.

"Then Dr. S put down the probe, applied more antiseptic to Jimmy's little penis and then massaged it to erection so that he could judge how much skin he should excise. He pulled Jimmy's foreskin forward so that it again – for the last time – covered his glans and picked up from his instrument table the traditional flat metal shield used by mohels for hundreds of years. He quickly pulled Jimmy's foreskin through the slit in the shield and adjusted the shield so that it lay parallel to the angle which the base of the glans makes with the shaft of the penis. Working with great speed he picked up a scalpel and, using the upper surface of the shield as his guide, sliced through the foreskin and then, having discarded the shield, he used the scalpel to trim away the remains of the inner layer of the foreskin still partially covering the glans so that the glans was fully bared. Finally he trimmed away the frenulum.

"It had seemed an age to me, but Judith told me later that she was sure the whole procedure took less than 3 minutes start to finish. She said ritual circumcisions were a little quicker but Dr. S had to remove Jimmy's frenulum as well and that was not part of the ritual operation. Although clearly exhausted, Jimmy was still crying as Dr. S applied antiseptic and Vaseline and bandaged him. Judith continued to keep the brandy-soused sugar cube between his lips as he was bandaged and I put his nappy back on. Then, after asking if I wanted to carry him into the bedroom or whether she should take him there, she handed him to me and followed D and me into the bedroom.

"As I wanted to give my poor little Jimmy the comfort of my breast as soon as possible after his ordeal was over, I had chosen for the occasion a dress with a quickly detachable top and I sat down on the bed and gave Jimmy my breast. He quietened down immediately and got to work like the good trencherman he is, which I found very reassuring after what he had been through. Judith and David went out to join the others for a drink, which I suspect most needed.

"After Jimmy had been fed he quickly fell asleep and after checking for any signs of bleeding I put him down in his cot and went back into the living room to be with the others. The grandmothers, plainly relieved it was all over, were comparing notes on similar occasions in the past – experiences with my brothers and David were being recalled - and I was commended for my valiant bearing. So was David who by then was looking much better than he had done earlier. While his mother was reminiscing about his circumcision I deliberately caught his eye and gave him a big, big smile trying to convey to him and hoping he would understand how much I felt I had benefited from it. He smiled back at me – message understood. Judith, perceptive as ever, caught the exchange and smiled broadly at me, sharing, it struck me, the thought that we each had a circumcised husband and today I had joined her as a mother of a circumcised son. I had joined the Sisterhood!

"Dr. Silverstein was preparing to leave and D and I thanked him for what we knew was expertly performed surgery. I told him it might be some time before we needed his services again but when the occasion arose we would be calling on him again. After he left, Anne said she and Mum had been discussing something as they drove to our house; they realized that we had had an expensive time recently and they wanted to pay Dr. S's fee so that they, as Jimmy's grandparents, could feel that they were contributing to carrying on a tradition shared by both families. This in addition to all the lovely baby clothes and equipment both sets of grandparents had already given us! D and I thought it was a beautiful idea, and we accepted and thanked them. Mum and Anne went away, as they had arrived, together – another nice piece of symbolism of the unity of our families.

"After the grannies left Judith handed me a beautifully wrapped little package and said it was a present for Jimmy. I opened it and found a most lovely silver mug inscribed with Jimmy's full name, "with love from Judith" and today's date. Judith said, a little worriedly I could sense, that she hoped D and I wouldn't mind. She knew from working during her school holidays in her father's jewellery shop that children were given christening mugs by their godparents, but she knew D's and my attitude towards religion and figured that Jimmy wouldn't be getting a christening or any presents from godparents. D and I had asked her to take an interest in Jimmy's welfare should anything untoward happen to us before he was old enough to fend for himself so she was already a sort of non-religious godmother, anyway. Besides that, she had held Jimmy on her lap for his circumcision just like the sandek or godfather would have held him at a bris, and didn't goyim – she corrected herself – gentiles, sometimes call a bris a christening with a knife? Anyway, godmother or not, she wanted to give Jimmy a present and here it was. She would leave it up to me to explain to Jimmy when he asked the significance of the date, but – here a typically wicked Judith-style grin appeared - if she suspected that he had not been told by the time he was 21 she reserved the right to spill the beans on her part in his remodelling! A typically thoughtful and kind gesture by my closest friend who really is a godmother of the very best sort and I know will look after Jimmy as her own if the need ever arises.

"As we thanked Judith for this lovely present the recipient awoke. He began to cry – the wound must have been hurting him, poor little fellow - and I put him to my breast again as quickly as I could for a mini-feed - a top up really, I suppose - as it wasn't that long since I had fed him. Judith checked his dressing for bleeding – OK. He went back to sleep immediately he stopped sucking and I put him down in his cot in our bedroom. Judith said that if he was like Michael after his bris he would sleep right through the afternoon and into the evening, adding that she thought it was nature's way of coping with the trauma he had endured, but that we could expect a disturbed night. She and I went back into the living room to have coffee with D before she went home. Judith, of course, had previous experience and had warned me of the psychological trauma which a bris inflicts on the baby's father, but D now appeared fully recovered, so much so in fact, that he was now eyeing me in the familiar speculative way that means that he is thinking about making love to me and wondering how soon the fun can begin. Judith, who is, as I have said before in this diary, a perceptive girl, admitted later that she observed and identified the look – it is similar to her own husband Mo's expression when he experiences the same urge. Thoughtful girl that she is, she took it as a signal to swallow the rest of her coffee, make her adieux and leave immediately! She had arranged for Michael to spend the day with her mother and Mo was coming home for lunch – which must have been by design as she, like me, thinks of circumcision as an act of sexual preparation; to both of us the act of permanently baring a boy's glans is a blatant preparation for future sexual intercourse. Judith and I had admitted to each other long ago that this consideration made any young male's circumcision, whether a bris or non-religious, sexually stimulating, so we both knew that each of us would be thinking of our own pressing sexual needs. So it didn't surprise me when Judith said she must be on her way home to get Mo's lunch ready. D and I thanked her for the wonderful support and help she had given us that morning and thanked her again for Jimmy's silver mug. She said she would pop round next morning to help with Jimmy when Dr S made his check-up visit. She disappeared bidding us "Bye, kiddos, make the best of it before he wakes up and don't get up to anything I wouldn't do," as she went through the front door.

"It's great to have a friend like Judith. We confide in each other a lot and she's always ready to give a helping hand. Today I had needed her help and moral support as never before and she gave both in full measure and unstintingly. As she left I hoped her needs would be satisfied by Mo as adequately as I hoped D would satisfy mine. I doubted that Mo was going to get much lunch.

"I caught D's eye and had no more difficulty in reading the signal he was transmitting than Judith had a few minutes before, so I said, "Okay, David, I need it too. I don't just want it. I really do need it. Let's go." We exchanged a long, lingering kiss in the living room before I led him by the hand into our bedroom. I remarked that we'd been through something together which was both an ordeal and an event to celebrate. Our first-born, our son, had suffered great pain but it was short term pain for long term gain and, like D, he had been prepared properly for his future role as a husband and lover, and this meant that he now looked like his father which was important to me as it bonded us together as a trio. I told D I was relieved it was all over safely but that it had turned me on and I needed all the love, comfort and sexual release only he could give me. D responded by saying that he had found the surgery and Jimmy's suffering and screaming hard to take – it had been much worse than he had expected – but now it was all over he needed me like I had said I needed him. The quick release dress I was wearing now came into its own again as D's eager hands made short work of removing it and it lay with my knickers round my ankles as I unbuckled D's belt and unzipped him to reveal an almighty bulge in his underpants – luckily the trauma he had so recently experienced had not had any deleterious effect on the part which was most vulnerable, psychologically speaking. Totally nude now, I kicked my dress and knickers away from me and got D's underpants off to reveal a truly splendid erection. Just what I needed. He picked me up and laid me gently on the bed before joining me there. I felt so very sensuous and full of sexual desire.

"I often have an overwhelming urge to take D's cock into my mouth but today it was stronger than ever and I lapped my tongue all over it before teasing him by running my fingernail right round it just below the throbbing head, a symbolic reminder of the bonding between him and Jimmy and me which we had witnessed this morning. D's penis went even harder - rock hard. Luckily I was very moist. The lovemaking which followed was the wildest, most loving and, to be honest, most lustful I have ever experienced and I think it was because we were both relieved that Jimmy's ordeal was over as well as very much turned on sexually by the circumcision itself and its symbolism to us as a badge of membership of our little family unit.

"Jimmy slept on undisturbed by his parents' gyrations,

which were noisier than usual, and as predicted by Judith he slept through the afternoon and evening – the aftermath of surgical shock and brandy, I suppose. I hope he got some relief from the brandy, poor little thing. Jimmy's long sleep and D's reluctant departure to his office this afternoon have allowed me to write this, my longest ever, diary entry. I wanted to complete it today before the details of the day faded from my mind. Judith phoned during the afternoon to see how Jimmy was doing and - she really is a wicked girl - to admit she left us so precipitately for two reasons; her own pressing sexual needs and her recognition of David's and mine. Dr. S is coming again tomorrow to check Jimmy and change the dressing."

Next day's diary entry read-

"C Day plus 1. We had rather a disturbed night, just as Judith predicted. Poor Jimmy had had a long sleep and when he woke up in the evening and I had checked his dressing for signs of any bleeding I fed him. Again he seemed to take comfort from being fed and cuddled but through the night he slept only fitfully and whenever he became restless or started to cry I picked him up and cuddled him and gave him mini-feeds at what seemed very frequent intervals. Poor David had to go to work today as usual, but he gallantly got up every time Jimmy cried. So none of us were our usual bright selves this morning. David got up to make early morning tea but was too worn out to do more than cuddle me and give me a kiss before breakfast – in contrast to yesterday's stellar performance. But before he left for the office he sneaked into the bathroom and using my lipstick he wrote "NORWICH" on the mirror. After he'd gone I found it and, thoroughly mystified, phoned him during the morning to ask what it was all about. He laughed in a rather sinister way and complained about how innocent some young brides were before saying it was something wartime servicemen used to write on the backs of envelopes containing letters to their wives and girlfriends. My father had been in the Navy during the war, hadn't he? Obviously my mother hadn't done a very good job of telling me the facts of life. Finally he explained it stood for "(K) Nickers Off Ready When I Come Home" and slammed down the phone still laughing. So I knew what to expect come 5.50 pm. Yippee!

"Judith arrived soon after my call to D and checked Jimmy's dressing as I had done at frequent intervals yesterday and this morning. I had time before Dr. S's visit to show her the message on the mirror. She couldn't guess what it meant so I had to translate. We had a good chortle before Dr. S arrived. When he removed the dressing I had my first real opportunity to study the result of his craftsmanship on Jimmy. Judith and I could see he had done a first class job. The incisions were neat and regular and Judith and I were satisfied that Jimmy should grow up with a very handsome penis with a fully exposed head, just enough skin to allow for erection and no frenulum. We both thought that Dr. S had done as good a job on my Jimmy as he had on her Michael.

"Pleased, I think, that we had complimented him on the surgery he had performed, Dr. S anointed Jimmy with more antiseptic and, to stop the dressing sticking to the wound as it healed, Vaseline and applied a new dressing. The procedure had disturbed Jimmy – no wonder, poor little thing - and he cried until the rebandaging was finished. I put him to my breast as Dr. S left.

"Judith sat with me as I fed and cuddled my baby. I was a bit upset and wept a little – reaction, I suppose, to the trauma suffered by Jimmy during the last 24 hrs - and, sensitive to my mood and knowing I needed cheering up, Judith regaled me with a thoroughly ribald, blow-by-blow account of Mo's alleged lunch-time yesterday. She admitted to feeling randy as she waited for his arrival and to wondering what D and I were doing to each other – which made her feel randier! I don't think Mo had realized why Judith had suggested that he should come home for lunch that day, but while engaged in tearing his business suit and shirt off him in the entrance hall, she explained that she was very much in love with him and couldn't wait until the evening and then pushed him into the bedroom. The sex was good, she said, very good indeed, but by the time her immediate needs were satisfied there was no time for Mo to eat if he was to get back to his office in time for his first afternoon appointment. So he went back to work hungry but, she thought, happy. She gave him a hastily prepared chopped liver sandwich to consume in the car en route to his office. When he came home in the evening, he said he had no complaints about his lunch break, but asked why she had acted like a woman possessed instead of a housewife and mother, so she had had to explain that she and I had been through a traumatic morning together and were both in urgent need of conjugal love and support from our respective spouses. She was glad to be able to say that after Michael had been put to bed, Mo and she "had got back together again" - as, with unusual delicacy, she put it - and she had felt quite restored and slept like a log – "a well satisfied log, that is," she said with a laugh.

"Judith's account of "lunch" with Mo gave me lots of laughs and bucked me up no end, and I felt even better by the time I finished telling her how D and I had gone about comforting each other. I appreciated once again what a good friend I have in her.

"I'm glad I've now had a proper look at Jimmy's remodelled widdler and relieved that Judith, who has had more experience of newborn circumcisions than I, thinks as I do that his surgery was excellently performed. When Judith invited me to assist at Michael's bris even though I'm not Jewish, I took it as a very special demonstration of our friendship. I feel so glad I have a friend like her who will rally round and give expert advice when I most need it as I did when arranging Jimmy's circumcision, and support me before, during and after the op as she has selflessly done.

"It's nearly time for D to arrive from the office. I've fed Jimmy and put him down to sleep, prepared supper and I'm going to have a quick shower. As instructed I am going to leave my nether garment off! When D gets home we'll find out if this morning's message on the mirror was the serious statement of intent I hope it was."

A week later, Kate's diary entry read –

"C Day plus 7. Jimmy has been having sponge baths since

his circumcision, but as his wound has healed so well I bathed him in the basin this morning. While I was washing him he developed a cute little erection proving he's all boy. I took a good look while he was enjoying his bath. Dr. S has done a really splendid job on him and he has a very good-looking penis with a well shaped head (I nearly said pretty, but that won't do). The glans and corona are totally exposed, there is no bunched skin below the glans or surplus skin on the shaft, the frenulum has been neatly removed and the scar line is neat and regular and looks set to disappear completely, so the result is a perfect circumcision, surgically and cosmetically. Enough to make any mum proud and happy to remove his nappy and show him off!

"As I make this diary entry it strikes me that in the fourteen days since I passed my six week check up, D and I have made love every morning and evening except only the morning of C Day plus 1 when we had had an almost sleepless night. I have taken his NORWICH message to heart and whenever circs permitted he has come home to a wife sans cullotte.

"During the morning the young – well, younger than me – health visitor made her second monthly visit to check on Jimmy's progress. I wish I liked her more than I do. I still hadn't let on that I'm a nurse. She was happy enough with his weight gain, but much less happy when she undressed him before weighing him. I was watching her expression closely as she took his nappy off and, just as I expected, a distinct look of displeasure, beyond a mere frown, was clearly visible before she spoke when she adopted a tone of reproof. "I see that since my last visit your baby has been circumcised. You did not ask my advice before the operation and I wish you had. When I visited you I mentioned that, as is quite normal at his age, his prepuce was not retractable but it was not interfering with his urinating and I told you that his foreskin was not a matter for any concern unless it was still not retractable at the age of six years when he could be assessed to see if treatment by stretching the opening of the prepuce or, as a final resort only, circumcision was advisable. I know from our records that he is not Jewish or Moslem. Your baby did not need to have the circumcision which has been performed on him. If it is not necessary, it is a mutilating procedure as well as being painful. I am sorry that you saw fit to have it done. May I ask why?"

"Her manner was not free from the arrogance one unfortunately finds in some professionals dealing with non-professionals like she obviously assumed I was and both her manner and her spoutings straight from the welfare state and NHS bible had riled me, so I decided to have some fun. I noticed she wasn't wearing a wedding ring so she probably isn't married. She may or may not be a virgin. "Well," I said, "my husband is circumcised and never complains about it. He gives me very good orgasms every time we make love, so I know that his circumcision has certainly not impaired his capability to satisfy me and, so far from being mutilated, I think a circumcised penis looks much nicer than an intact one. I will ask him when he comes home whether he feels he has been mutilated and advise you of his answer when you next call." She was plainly shocked at being so addressed, but came back saying that the NHS had determined that circumcisions were rarely necessary and certainly not in my son's case. I responded by saying, "In general I don't think one should argue with success. My experience with my husband's circumcised state including his performance in bed is such that I wanted my future daughter-in-law to experience sexual satisfaction similar to that regularly given me by my circumcised husband. Furthermore, I wanted my son to have the health, hygienic, sexual and aesthetic advantages of circumcision."

"Then the HV asked me what medical advice had been obtained before Jimmy's circumcision. "Oh," I said, "I discussed it with my mother-in-law and my mother and we all thought it was better for him to be done." She retorted that she had asked what medical advice had been taken (with heavy emphasis on the word"medical"). "I heard what you said. My mother-in-law is a practising surgeon and general practitioner with a family practice, my mother was an operating theatre sister at the Royal Infirmary and, when not on maternity leave, I'm a senior operating theatre nurse at the Royal Infirmary. We discussed the issue very thoroughly and all three of us considered that Jimmy's long term interests were best served by his undergoing a circumcision. You have expounded to me the NHS position that circumcision is almost always unnecessary and that it is a mutilating and painful, even barbaric, operation. All three of us as experienced professionals are very well aware of and totally disagree with the NHS doctrine which we believe is based on a desire to save money rather than on any intention to provide the best medical care available. You probably know that routine infant circumcision is practised on about 90% of boys born in the USA, but do you realize that all royal princes are still circumcised and that the Queen followed the tradition of having Prince Charles circumcised by the senior mohel of the London Jewish congregation rather than follow NHS doctrine on the fate of the royal foreskin?" The HV moved hurriedly to nutritional matters. Although I gave her coffee and biscuits before she left, I don't think she much enjoyed her visit. I hope that the next time she is presented with an exposed glans penis she will not lambaste the unfortunate mother, but she struck me as earnest, puritanical, arrogant and doctrinaire. I am still wondering if she has any practical knowledge of the male organ of copulation. Maybe a little practical debauchery should be added as a compulsory element in the HV training course. Memo: ask David if he has been mutilated and make a note of his response."

Two weeks later, Kate wrote in her diary-

"Now that Jimmy's wound has healed we had a Sunday morning bath en famille, all three of us, for the first time. Comparing the large and small male organs on display, I remarked to D that twenty-odd years ago he had gone through the pain of being made ready with a knife for some unknown future wife who turned out to be me and now Jimmy had been through the same ordeal for the benefit of another unknown future wife. "Lucky girl!" was D's irreverent rejoinder. Then he added, "And I am fortunate enough to know another lucky girl!" and gave me a big kiss on my lips and a less than respectful slap on my wet derriere."

Later that week Kate's diary entry read-

"Several of my closest friends were students at the nursing school and nurses at the Royal Infirmary with me and have asked when they could see the baby, so I invited them as a group for a buffet lunch at our house today. It was a thoroughly enjoyable affair as most of us don't see each other very often - several are working in hospitals other than the Royal Infirmary and some are full-time mums like lucky me. Some, like Marianne (who has identical twin sons), Judith and Margaret, had babies before I had Jimmy and they brought them along with them. Catherine, Stephanie, Joanna and Deborah were all there, too. Everyone knew each other well so conversation was lively and non-stop, a mixture of professional gossip and mum talk which all enjoyed.

"It was Margaret, my old mentor, who asked me if Jimmy had been circumcised. I answered that he had been done four weeks ago when he was 7 wks old and Margaret rejoined, "That does surprise me. Knowing how strongly you feel about circumcision I would never have thought he would have remained intact until you took him home from hospital and had to begin bathing him yourself. Why the delay?" Judith, who had been my salvation when Mum asked a similar question, caught my eye, but mischievously chose not to intervene this time, and instead began to laugh before I could formulate a credible if not entirely honest reply to this rather embarrassing question and Margaret turned to her inquiringly. "Well," said Judith, "it's like this. Kate wanted to celebrate the event in style and that meant waiting until she'd had her 6 week check-up." This, naturally, caused general laughter at my expense and some ribald remarks, so I said, "Okay, girls, mock me if you will, but it turned out to be a jolly good idea. Yes, I do believe that every baby boy should be circumcised but when it's one's own baby that is being done it's a bit nerve-wracking and by waiting until after my check-up David was able to help me through it by making love to me before and after Jimmy's op. It relaxed me and was far easier on me than being in hospital after the birth and having my baby taken away from me for his circumcision and lying in bed thinking about everything that might go wrong and waiting for him to be returned to me. I don't think it's any harder on a baby to be circumcised at 7 weeks than at 7 days, so I don't feel guilty about delaying it and if I have another son he will also have to wait till his Mum passes her 6 week check up."

"Margaret said she took my point and it was a very valid one. She remarked that after some serious string pulling to evade the NHS diktat against circumcision for non-medical reasons her son had been circumcised while she was still in the maternity wing after his birth. The surgeon who did it was a personal friend and I had assisted him. She had always been determined that any son of hers would be circumcised but when it came to handing the baby over to me to take him down for the op she had been like every other mother, only worse. It had been very upsetting, even though the surgeon and nurse were not strangers but personal friends whom she trusted implicitly, and she, a theatre nurse herself, had been in tears when she gave me her baby and at times while she waited for me to bring him back. If she had another baby boy she would seriously think about a circumcision at home when she had got over the birth. She very kindly called it the Kate Gambit.

"Judith commented that attending Jimmy's circumcision had been a big contrast to her own son Michael's bris which she had had to arrange for the 8th day after his birth. While still exhausted from the birth she had to plan and organize both the surgery and a reception for her family and her husband's family and their friends. She felt absolutely pooped when the last guest departed and she was left with a distressed baby to care for. She envied my freedom to arrange Jimmy's circumcision at a time and in a manner of my own choice.

"Stephanie, who is expecting her first baby, asked if she could see Jimmy without his nappy. All the girls gathered round to view Dr. Silverstein's craftsmanship and gave it a thumbs up. Stephanie thanked me and asked for Dr. S's phone number. If she has a baby boy he will be circumcised and she will ask Dr. S to do it. Marianne told me that Dr. S had circumcised her twins and she and her husband (a doctor) had been very pleased with the neatness of the surgery on both her boys."

Several months later Kate confided to her diary-

"John phoned from Canada to say that Jean had a "perfect" 7 1/2lb son today. Both well. So I'm now an aunt. Those two haven't wasted any time. It's only eleven months since they married and promptly emigrated."

"Mum round. Pleased to be a grandmother of two now, this time courtesy of Jean and John. She has been on the phone to Jean in hospital as well as John – Dad's phone bill will be horrendous. She was giggling as she told me, but I think very pleased as well as amused to hear via John, that when Jean's paediatrician – one of John's partners in the medical practice - dropped by Jean's hospital room to report to her on his first examination of the baby, even before he had time to begin his report, the very first thing she did was to ask him when he would circumcise her son. Mum, who is very fond of Jean, made the point that Jean had asked "when", not "if," and claimed that it proved she'd done a good job in educating her daughter-in-law. "Maybe a better job with Jean than with my own daughter," she added, and commented pointedly that "Jean's son will lose his unnecessary appendage before he's a week old in contrast to Jimmy who had to wait for seven weeks before his dilatory mother got around to attending to the matter." I stayed quiet about the reason for the delay, but I shall never regret it – the sheer intensity of our lovemaking that day and the comfort it gave me was something never to be forgotten. When we made love that morning before we got up it strengthened me for Jimmy's forthcoming ordeal and reassured me as nothing else could have done that we were doing the right thing for our son. When we made love afterwards as Jimmy slept, we both got the mutual comforting and intense sexual release we needed. My new nephew's hospital circumcision will be a sterile, impersonal affair as compared with the loving family setting of Jimmy's with his parents and grandmothers around him to support him. And I can't help thinking that while the day was a memorable and happy occasion, as one looks back, for D and me, it will be no occasion at all for Jean and John.

"I have just re-read what I wrote about the day of Jimmy's

circumcision and D and I making love beforehand and afterwards. When I'm an old lady I'm going to be glad I was so explicit in how I've described our lovemaking on that occasion and many other times in this diary. I hope D will enjoy reading it, when I allow him to do so, as much as I expect to enjoy re-reading it myself. Better still, I'm going to enjoy reading my diary to D when we are both old age pensioners sitting in our rocking chairs. I do hope we will still be sexually active as long as we live."

A few weeks later another entry in Kate's diary read –

"Today was another day when passion took over – happily, it seems to happen quite often even though we are an old married couple – but for some reason our lovemaking today was something special in intensity of feeling and memorable. Maybe it was the sheer sensuality of it all. I know I was thinking of that magic day when I lost my virginity – a day which started with me, a rather modest girl really, then as now, leaving my panties off with a view to D discovering the omission and taking advantage of me. Ha, ha! Who in our household takes advantage of whom?

"Be that as it may, I bathed Jimmy, fed him and put him down to sleep ahead of the time D would be coming home from work – it was his half day off from the office and I hoped he would spend it in bed with me. All morning as I did the household chores and cared for Jimmy, I had been feeling randy and thinking how much I needed D's very stiff and aroused cock inside me to give me the release I craved and I kept visualizing pulling his pants down to reveal a raging erection ready to give me the satisfaction I wanted so badly. Although I was busy the morning seemed interminable. After I put Jimmy in his cot, on a sudden impulse I took Mum's old kitchen chair of happy memory up to our bedroom and placed it inconspicuously by the wardrobe. Then I showered and prettied myself up and put on that same old halter-top sun dress which had played its part in my downfall years ago before we got officially engaged. Again I put on a pair of panties and, having put them on, again I thought no! – not when I'm feeling so randy - and I slipped them off just as D's car crunched the gravel in our driveway. I went downstairs in time to greet him in the hall as he entered the house and, how history repeats itself, he kissed me, ran his hand up my leg under my dress and stopped. "Great," he said, "upstairs with you, woman. NOW!" and slapped my behind to hasten me on my way. Upstairs, we undressed each other and D said he needed a pee. He went into the bathroom and I, no longer the innocent modest Kate of the pre-David era, followed him. He raised the lavatory seat – well trained is my David – not realizing I was just behind him. I reached in front of him to grasp his prized organ – I prize it, too – just as he started to pee and felt my usual pleasure in aiming the flow for him. When he finished peeing I grasped the skin covering his shaft just below the head, pulled it back as far as it would go – which isn't far - and began to move it back and forth, knowing the pleasure he always gets from such personal attention. The result was an immediate and very impressive erection. Then, as my needs were immediate and did not allow of my chivvying D into the shower before he satisfied them, I said "I'm a nurse, you know, and I can't allow you entrance to my boudoir unless you agree to be properly washed in all relevant areas." I filled a small basin with warm water, grabbed the soap and marched him into the bedroom. Confident he was going to enjoy whatever was on offer, he lay down on the bed with some alacrity and an already impressive erection. Using an old nursing trick I gave his flagstaff a sharp tap with the edge of my hand to cool things down while I performed my professional duty as a nurse, but the resulting tumescence was short lived. For good measure I grabbed my student nurse headgear from the top of the wardrobe and plonked it on my head. I wonder if matrons know what useful erotic props they equip their (sometimes) virginal charges with? I proceeded to examine, manipulate, soap and rinse his equipment – which gave equal pleasure to giver and receiver alike, I think - and exercised all prerogatives due to a wife and nurse, finishing up by licking him dry.

"This afternoon, as we sometimes do when we are enjoying a set-piece sexual encounter – i.e. one premeditated by one or both of us, as opposed to one which just happens when we are in bed – I included as a curtain raiser before intercourse a charade we both enjoy. Using the contents of my manicure set as instruments and a little shield like Dr. S's which I made out of plastic, I pretend to circumcise my already very thoroughly circumcised husband. I start by plonking between his lips a piece of sugar wrapped in gauze and soused in his own brandy (prepared just before he came home) – like Jimmy did, he sucks really happily on this. Then, with more imagination than reality, I pull as much skin as I can manoeuvre over the corona of his glans - and since he was tightly and neatly circumcised and is erect, this requires imagination. I take a blunted manicure instrument which is a reasonable facsimile of a probe and pass it between his glans and the miniscule remnant of his foreskin, pretending to separate the adhesions between the glans and foreskin. Then, with the shield held at the correct angle, I pretend to pull his foreskin through the slit in the shield and with the most theatrical sweep of my nail file (masquerading as a scalpel) I can muster, I "remove" his foreskin. Then I use the ersatz scalpel to trim away the inner part of the foreskin which (in theory!) is still covering part of his glans. He doesn't get bandaged because he has by now developed a raging hard-on and we are both more than ready for the main course. After kissing his penis better and wishing it a quick recovery from the surgery I have just performed on it I join him on the bed. By now I am very aroused too and lie with my legs apart ready for D to enter me but as he moves into position above me I grasp his cock and pull the skin covering his shaft back as far as I can and run my forefinger nail right round his cock just below the head and remind him that I love his being a roundhead. Then, hoping against hope that Jimmy will co-operate by remaining asleep until we've had at least one good orgasm apiece, I guide D's cock into me and we make love.

"That afternoon we had completed the charade and I was about to get in bed with him when D suddenly noticed the old chair. He is at least as fond of that antique as I am and for the same reasons. He began a wild whoop but suppressed it remembering the pressing need to keep quiet if Jimmy was not to wake and bring our lovemaking to a premature, and unsatisfying/unsatisfied, end. He laughed and getting off the bed, grabbed me and sat down on the old chair with a very erect cock indeed, the glans very prominent and the skin covering the shaft stretched taut. I knelt in front of him facing a very respectable – if that is the right word – erection and took as much of it as I could accommodate into my mouth. Memories of my being deflowered by that penis as I straddled that chair came flooding – literally, as I now felt very wet - back to me. This time I didn't need any artificial lubricant. I rose from the floor and stood momentarily straddling his thighs. I bent down and grasped his penis with my hand, encircling it with my thumb and forefinger immediately below the glans. I moved my hand downwards marvelling at how tightly stretched was the skin covering the shaft. It was physical evidence, if any were needed, that D needed me as much as I needed him. Guiding his throbbing penis into my waiting vagina as I lowered myself on to him, I felt his penis enter and fill my vagina. By bending and flexing my knees, I was able to raise and lower my torso enough to give his penis and my clitoris the stimulation they required and we both attained the orgasms we needed. Afterwards we relaxed, with me still astride D, and he with a great grin said that the ease with which I had impaled myself on his penis proved that I was no longer the virgin I had been the first time he'd sat in the old chair!"

FINALE

KATE'S CREDO

(A statement of belief found among Kate's writings)

"I believe that in choosing to circumcise her son - and it is usually the mother who makes that choice - a mother is consciously or unconsciously preparing him for sexual intercourse. The permanent baring of the glans penis effected by circumcision is, I think, a blatant readying of him for his future sexual role, reflecting a woman's instinctive preference for a penis which always looks ready for the act of coition.

"I recommend circumcision of the male because –

it improves hygiene for the male, eliminating penile cancer and a potential source of odour;

it improves hygiene for the female partner, reducing the risk of her developing cervical cancer;

it improves the female partner's ability to attain orgasm for three reasons –
first, the glans penis permanently and completely bared by circumcision becomes less sensitive due to keratinisation through its exposure to friction from clothing, an effect that results in a slowing down of the male's orgasm - a factor in lengthening the duration of intercourse and thus favouring attainment by the female of her orgasm,
secondly, inside the vagina the corona of the glans of a

fully circumcised penis is always in direct contact with the wall of the vagina, there being no foreskin to interpose itself between the corona and the vaginal wall during movement of the penis up or down the vagina, and this gives the female greater stimulation, and thirdly, a glans not constrained by the presence of a foreskin tends to grow to be larger than one with a foreskin and consequently creates more sensation within the vagina; if performed in infancy, it eliminates any possible need for circumcision later in life when the operation is more complicated, expensive and inconvenient; andit improves the aesthetic appearance of the penis.

"Consequently I believe in routine infant circumcision, but freedom of individual choice means that it should never be made compulsory. It should always be a matter of parental choice. In this I differ from the National Health Service which has denied parents the right to elect that their child be circumcised.

"To obtain the maximum benefit it is important that a circumcision is fully and completely performed so that the glans and corona are left permanently bared and all redundant skin removed. Preferably the frenulum should also be excised.

"As a woman I have always found male circumcision a most erotic topic. The circumcised state of my husband and later my witnessing the circumcision of my baby son have given me deep and abiding satisfaction."